"Red Alert! We're under attack!"

The energy field absorbed the blow, but for a second the power blinked and the inertial dampers failed. The deck beneath Jake's feet shook.

On the beam, Riv gave a strangled cry of surprise and lost his footing.

Jake saw Riv stumble and then fall.

Then Kam flung herself forward. Her left hand wrapped around Riv's wrist, and her other encircled the beam. With a cry of pain, she fell forward across the beam.

Riv swung below her, high above the Promenade. Kam's face twisted in agony, and Jake saw that she was losing her grip on the beam. He jumped through the ceiling and out onto the beam. Behind him Nog gasped.

The thin beam sagged under Jake's additional weight. . . .

Star Trek: The Next Generation

Starfleet Academy

#1 Worf's First Adventure
#2 Line of Fire
#3 Survival
#4 Capture the Flag
#5 Atlantis Station

Star Trek: Deep Space Nine

#1 The Star Ghost
#2 Stowaways
#3 Prisoners of Peace

Available from MINSTREL Books

PRISONERS OF PEACE

JOHN PEEL

**Interior illustrations by
Todd Cameron Hamilton**

A MINSTREL® BOOK

PUBLISHED BY POCKET BOOKS

New York   London   Toronto   Sydney   Tokyo   Singapore

This book is a work of fiction. Names, characters, places and incidents are products of the author's imagination or are used fictitiously. Any resemblance to actual events or locales or persons, living or dead, is entirely coincidental.

A MINSTREL PAPERBACK *ORIGINAL*

A Minstrel Book published by
POCKET BOOKS, a division of Simon & Schuster Inc.
1230 Avenue of the Americas, New York, NY 10020

STAR TREK is a Registered Trademark of
® Paramount Pictures.

This book is published by Pocket Books, a division of Simon & Schuster Inc., under exclusive license from Paramount Pictures.

ISBN: 0-671-88288-0

First Minstrel Books printing October 1994

10 9 8 7 6 5 4 3 2 1

A MINSTREL BOOK and colophon are registered trademarks of Simon & Schuster Inc.

Cover art by Alan Gutierrez

Printed in the U.S.A.

For Donna Chisholm

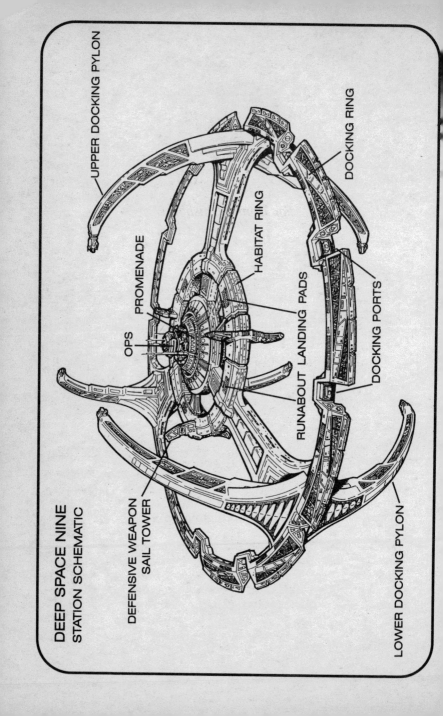

DEEP SPACE NINE
STATION SCHEMATIC

UPPER DOCKING PYLON

DOCKING RING

HABITAT RING

PROMENADE

OPS

DOCKING PORTS

RUNABOUT LANDING PADS

DEFENSIVE WEAPON
SAIL TOWER

LOWER DOCKING PYLON

STAR TREK®: DEEP SPACE NINE™
Cast of Characters

JAKE SISKO—Jake is a young teenager and the only human boy permanently on board Deep Space Nine. Jake's mother died when he was very young. He came to the space station with his father but found very few kids his own age. He doesn't remember life on Earth, but he loves baseball and candy bars, and he hates homework. His father doesn't approve of his friendship with Nog.

NOG—He is a Ferengi boy whose primary goal in life—like all Ferengi—is to make money. His father, Rom, is frequently away on business, which is fine with Nog. His uncle, Quark, keeps an eye on him. Nog thinks humans are odd with their notions of trust and favors and friendship. He doesn't always understand Jake, but since his father forbids him to hang out with the human boy, Nog and Jake are best friends. Nog loves to play tricks on people, but he tries to avoid Odo whenever possible.

COMMANDER BENJAMIN SISKO—Jake's father has been appointed by Starfleet Command to oversee the operations of the space station and act as a liaison between the Federation and Bajor. His wife was killed in a Borg attack, and he is raising Jake by himself. He is a very busy man who always tries to make time for his son.

ODO—The security officer was found by Bajoran scientists years ago, but Odo has no idea where he originally came from. He is a shape-shifter, and thus can assume any shape for a period of time. He normally maintains a vaguely human appearance but every sixteen hours he must revert to his natural liquid state. He has no patience for lawbreakers and less for Ferengi.

MAJOR KIRA NERYS—Kira was a freedom fighter in the Bajoran underground during the Cardassian occupation of Bajor. She now represents Bajoran interests aboard the station and is Sisko's first officer. Her temper is legendary.

LIEUTENANT JADZIA DAX—An old friend of Commander Sisko's, the science officer Dax is actually two joined entities known as the Trill. There is a separate consciousness—a symbiont—in the young female host's body. Sisko knew the symbiont Dax in a previous host, which was a "he."

DR. JULIAN BASHIR—Eager for adventure, Doctor Bashir graduated at the top of his class and requested a deep-space posting. His enthusiasm sometimes gets him into trouble.

MILES O'BRIEN—Formerly the Transporter Chief aboard the *U.S.S. Enterprise,* O'Brien is now Chief of Operations on Deep Space Nine.

KEIKO O'BRIEN—Keiko was a botanist on the *Enterprise,* but she moved to the station with her husband and her young daughter, Molly. Since there is little use for her botany skills on the station, she is the teacher for all of the permanent and traveling students.

QUARK—Nog's uncle and a Ferengi businessman by trade, Quark runs his own combination restaurant/casino/holosuite venue on the Promenade, the central meeting place for much of the activity on the station. Quark has his hand in every deal on board and usually manages to stay just one step ahead of the law—usually in the shape of Odo.

PRISONERS
OF PEACE

CHAPTER 1

I sn't that the most awesome thing you've ever seen?" asked Jake Sisko. He was standing at one of the large windows on the Upper Level of the Promenade, staring out into space. There was an endless fascination for him in looking at the stars. Other people and alien beings found the view just as attractive. Scattered along the Upper Level were a dozen or so individuals either staring or just glancing out at the view.

At that moment, though, there was much more than simply stars to be seen. Deep Space Nine—the space station Jake and hundreds of other humans, Bajorans, and other species lived on—was situated on the edge of the Denorios asteroid belt in the Bajoran solar system. The station was here because of the wormhole.

It was kind of hard to grasp exactly what the wormhole was. It was some kind of tunnel punched through subspace, joining this spot in the Bajoran system with one almost half a galaxy away. Passing through the wormhole in a matter of minutes, a spaceship could cross from Bajor to the Gamma Quadrant—a voyage that would normally take even a powerful starship like the *U.S.S. Enterprise* more than seventy years to make at top warp speed. Most of the time the wormhole was invisible to the eye, but when a ship passed through, it became suddenly and spectacularly visible. It was as if a huge, sparkling whirlpool was spinning in space, glowing and pulsing with all the colors ever imagined—and then some. The tunnel itself would spring into being, and then the ship traveling through the wormhole would fly toward the station. In a flurry of color the wormhole would fold in on itself and vanish.

Jake had just seen this happen as a freighter came through the glowing web of colors. It was spectacular, and he felt a thrill just watching it. "Isn't that the most awesome thing you've ever seen?" he repeated when his best friend didn't answer.

"Huh?" Nog dragged his eyes up and glanced out the window. His face broke into a fang-filled grin. "It sure is," he agreed. "A Bajoran trade ship! Loaded with goods, too, by the look of the way it's moving." He rubbed his hands together. "This means a chance to make some money."

Jake sighed. Trust Nog to think he'd been talking about money and not beauty! He liked Nog a lot, but there were times when he wondered why. Nog was a Ferengi boy, the same age as Jake, but apart from that they couldn't have been less alike. Jake was tall, slim, and dark-skinned. He generally wore a jumpsuit. Nog was short, by human standards, and definitely took some getting used to if you hadn't seen a Ferengi before.

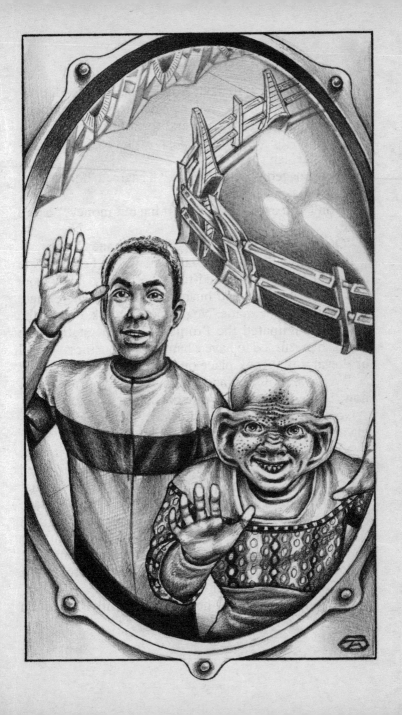

Huge, ridged ears jutted out from his hairless head. Bony lumps and thick brow ridges made his head look over-large. His clothing was rich and form-fitting.

"I meant the wormhole," Jake explained. "It's really spectacular, isn't it?"

Nog shrugged. "Yeah, I guess," he agreed, bored. "But *we* can't make a profit off it."

"Don't you ever think of anything but money?" asked Jake.

"Of course I do!" said Nog. *"More* money."

It wasn't really his fault, Jake knew. The Ferengi were a race of beings who lived to make money. They were merchants, traders, and businessbeings anywhere there was a profit to be made. Nog's uncle, Quark, owned the bar that dominated the Promenade of the station. He was also presumed to have a hand in any business—legal or illegal—that took place on Deep Space Nine.

"Well, we're not going to be making any profits right now," Jake told him. "We've got to get to school."

Nog scowled. "Let's play hockey," he suggested, staring at the approaching freighter.

"I think you mean *hookey,*" Jake told him, grinning. "Don't you remember that Ms. O'Brien said she'd tell your uncle if you didn't turn up? And you know what *he'll* do to you." Keiko O'Brien was their teacher. Jake liked her, and she seemed to enjoy tutoring the small class. Nog, however, was a bit of a problem student. For one thing, Ferengi didn't like women telling them what to do. For another, they were easily distracted from their lessons by the thought of money.

Nog winced. "Yeah," he said reluctantly. "And I'd

look pretty stupid if he *did* rip off one of my ears and made me eat it, wouldn't I?" As they started off for the schoolroom, he added: "Do you think he *really* means it?"

"I don't know," Jake answered. "But we could always find out by not showing up. You want to risk an ear on that?"

Nog clutched at his ear protectively. Ferengi were very vain about their huge ears, which were very sensitive. "No way!"

"I didn't think so." Jake privately didn't believe Quark meant his threat, but if it kept Nog attending school, he was willing to play along with it. Actually, Jake knew from what his father had said that Quark didn't exactly like Nog being educated at all, let alone by humans. But Quark—like all Ferengi—was a business-man, and he could see the advantages to having someone around who understood human ways of thinking. Espe-cially if that someone was a person in his family. It would make it so much easier to take advantage of his human customers!

Jake actually enjoyed school for the most part. Ms. O'Brien hadn't always been a teacher—she'd been a botanist specializing in alien plant life when she and her husband had served on the *U.S.S. Enterprise.* This meant that she could tell some really great, true stories, and often explain the lessons by telling them of her own adventures. It made the lessons more interesting.

He and Nog were the last to arrive. There were only a dozen students in the class, and Jake was the oldest. The youngest was six years old. Apart from Nog, there were only two of the other students that Jake felt were okay—a human girl named Ashley Fontana and a Vulcan girl named T'Ara. The rest were just too young.

Ashley was a tall, ten-year-old with long blond hair that hung halfway down her back. Her mother was a Technician who worked with Ms. O'Brien's husband. Ashley idolized her mother and was determined to be a Tech when she grew up. As a result, she loved taking things apart and trying to repair them. There were plenty of machines on Deep Space Nine that broke down often. It had been built by the Cardassians after they had conquered the planet Bajor, but it hadn't been built very well. Ashley was actually pretty good at fixing things, even if she wasn't as brilliant as she sometimes thought she was.

T'Ara was very different. She was only seven years old, but because she was a Vulcan she acted much older. Jake knew that Vulcans matured mentally much faster than humans did, so T'Ara was pretty much on a level with him, Nog, and Ashley. On the other hand, she took a bit of getting used to sometimes. The Vulcans believed that showing emotions was wrong, and that it interfered with things too much. Instead, they used mental exercises to bury their emotions and tried to live their lives on the system of logic. T'Ara was still young enough to forget her training sometimes, and she would let her emotions out. Then she'd be all embarrassed and ashamed of herself. Most of the time, though, she was okay. Like many Vulcans, she had dark hair, cut straight across her forehead, shaped around her pointed ears, and then cut short at the neck. Her eyebrows were slanted upward from the top of her nose.

Jake and Nog slipped quietly into their seats in front of the two girls. Ms. O'Brien looked at them but said nothing as they both activated the keypads to their computers. The teacher stood at the front of the class, with a newcomer beside her. Jake studied him with interest.

He was obviously a Bajoran boy—the ridges across the bridge of his nose made that quite clear, and the large earring in his right ear was the final proof. All the Bajorans seemed to love earrings. They wore them like badges or trophies. This boy looked to be about their age, and he had a sullen, bored expression on his thin face. He looked very skinny, as if he didn't eat very well. There was a faint white scar down the right side of his neck that vanished into the top of his clothing. His dark, curly hair looked as if it had been freshly cut. He looked as if he didn't want to be here.

"Now that everyone is here," Ms. O'Brien said carefully, "I'd like to introduce you all to Riv Jakar. He's just come aboard the station, and he's living with his uncle." She gave the boy one of her warm smiles. "Perhaps you'd like to tell us a bit about yourself, Riv?" she suggested.

Riv looked up, and then deliberately yawned. "No," he replied. "I don't want to be here, and I don't aim to stay." He glared around at the rest of the class. "And I sure don't want to get to know any of these *wimps.*" He sniffed. "What a bunch of losers."

Jake felt his face burning at this deliberate insult, but

he kept quiet. One of the Bajoran girls, Marn Laren, wasn't so restrained. Jumping to her feet, she glared at Riv, her face red and angry. "You'd better take that back," she snapped.

Riv just laughed. "Want to try and make me?" he taunted her.

"That's quite enough!" Ms. O'Brien stepped in front of Riv, then turned to glare at Marn. "Sit down," she ordered. For a moment it looked as if Marn wasn't going to, but then she scowled and slumped into her chair again. The teacher then turned to Riv. "That was deliberately rude," she said icily. "I won't tolerate that sort of thing in my class."

Not at all bothered by this, Riv shrugged. "So send me home," he suggested. "You don't want me here; I don't want to be here. So why don't I just go?"

"Because you're here to learn," Ms. O'Brien answered. "And the first thing you need to learn, I think, are some manners. You can't go around insulting your fellow students like that."

"They aren't anything like me," Riv said darkly. "Just look at them! Soft, fat, and lazy, that's what they are! I'll bet none of them ever had to hide from a Cardassian patrol or steal food just to stay alive."

"That's true," agreed Nog unexpectedly. "I steal food just because it's fun." He broke out laughing.

Riv scowled at this interruption. What seemed to annoy him most was that Jake and Ashley were trying not to giggle. Jake realized that the Bajoran boy didn't like the idea that they were trying to make fun of him.

Fighting back the laugh building up inside, Jake managed to ask: "Did *you* have to hide out, then?"

"Yes, I did," Riv said, his intense eyes daring them to laugh again—and earn a face full of fist. "My parents were both in the Bajoran underground. I was brought up fighting the Cardassians. None of you wimps ever did anything like that. While you were learning your ABCs, I was out there with a phaser fighting for my life!"

Jake was starting to see why Riv was so angry now.

He'd lived the life of a fugitive and never had a stable home. "So what happened to your parents?" he asked.

"My mother was killed in a raid," Riv replied. There was a lot of pain in his voice. "And the Cardassians caught my father. He died in a Cardassian jail. It took them three months to kill him." He fingered the thin chain hanging from his ear. "This was his once. It's all I have left to remember him by. He gave it to me just before he left on his last mission, to show that I was considered a *man*."

Jake felt sorry for him, but he could understand some of the boy's pain. "My mom was killed by the Borg," he said. "I know how hard it is. And now you're living with your uncle?"

"*Him?*" yelled Riv. "Only because I was forced to! *He* didn't fight for our planet! He's a coward and I hate him!" The Bajoran boy glared around the class. "And I hate all of you, too!"

CHAPTER 2

After a moment of embarrassed silence Ms. O'Brien said: "Well, I'm glad you're looking forward to class, Riv." There was a little laughter at this. "Right, I think you'd better sit over by Jake," she decided. Since there were plenty of empty desks, Jake realized she was doing this for a reason.

For a minute it looked as if Riv would refuse. Then he gave an elaborate shrug of his shoulders. "Yeah, why not?" he agreed. He slumped in the chair beside Jake.

"Thank you," the teacher said. "Now, can you operate the computer? If not, I'm sure Jake will be able to help you."

"I can do it," Riv snapped, glaring at Jake. "I don't need any help from anyone for anything." He punched the pad and the screen lit up. "See?"

"That's fine," said Ms. O'Brien. "Right, class, we're starting with biology today. I'd like you all to access the file material on the Gorn."

"I'd rather study Cardassian biology," grumbled Riv.

Jake grinned. "Is it interesting?" he asked.

"It could be," replied Riv. "I might be able to find a new way to kill one."

"That is *quite* enough," Ms. O'Brien said, firmly. "Riv, the war is over, and you have to learn to get on with your life, to make something of it."

"The only thing I want to do," Riv told her, "is to carry on what my parents started. I don't care about anything else but making the Cardassians pay for what they've done."

"There are other things in life," answered Ms. O'Brien. "You really should make an attempt to come to terms with that. But if you won't, then at least let the rest of the class learn."

Riv shrugged. "I don't care what they do."

"How kind," the teacher said. "Right, if you've all found the data files, you'll see that the Gorn are a reptile-like species first encountered . . ."

Jake tried to concentrate on the lesson, but his attention kept wandering back to Riv. The Bajoran boy was slouched over his desk, looking bored and annoyed. He obviously didn't want to be here. He was filled with anger and hurt. Jake could understand that. Riv must have lived for years on the run from the Cardassian soldiers—always tired, always hungry, and always in danger. He'd lost both his parents in the fighting and now was staying with an uncle he clearly despised. It was going to be hard for him to adjust to this new life— assuming he even wanted to try. It didn't look very likely at the moment.

At least Riv didn't disrupt the lessons further. He stayed sullen and silent for the rest of the morning. Finally it was time for lunch, and Ms. O'Brien called for the break.

Jake and Nog headed across to the small replicator unit in the corner of the room. Ashley and T'Ara went with them. Riv—trying to look uninterested—shambled along behind them.

"I hope this thing works right this time," Nog complained.

Ashley blushed. The food replicator in the classroom broke down almost every day. Ashley had insisted that she could repair it—and had tried six times so far. Chief O'Brien had allowed her to try because "she can't break it worse than it is, can she?" Every time the replicator was repaired, it broke down again.

"It's definitely right," she promised. "I stayed late after school yesterday and took it apart. I checked *everything*. It's definitely going to work right this time."

"That's what you said *yesterday,*" grumbled Nog. *"And* the day before."

"Yeah, well, maybe she got it fixed," Jake told his friend. Ashley was embarrassed enough by her constant failure; she didn't need Nog's complaints as well. "We'll give it a try." Standing in front of the machine, he addressed the computer. "Give me a soda, burger, and potatoes," he said.

There was a slight pause, and then a shimmering within the small chamber. On the ledge appeared a dish. . . .

"Oh, *gross!*" growled Riv. "What *is* that?"

Ashley blushed furiously, her whole face turning a bright red. "Stew and cheesecake," she hissed. *"Again."*

The Bajoran boy stared at it. "In one dish?" He stuck out his tongue in disgust. "I ate better than that when I scavenged on the garbage dumps for food."

"It is not supposed to produce that," T'Ara informed him.

"No kidding?" Riv laughed nastily at Ashley.

Ashley was too embarrassed by another failure to get too angry at this uncalled-for insult. "I don't understand it," she complained. "I was *sure* I'd fixed it."

"I understand it," Riv said. "You're just a useless idiot, like the others here."

"That's enough," Jake said, firmly. "Ashley's doing her best, so don't pick on her."

"You wanna make me?" challenged Riv, turning to face him. He looked eager for a fight. "Go ahead—try!"

Before Jake could react, Ms. O'Brien stepped forward. "There will be no fighting in my class," she said. "Riv, please keep from insulting everyone. Jake, maybe you and Nog could go to the replicator in my office and get lunch for everyone?"

Jake glared at Riv, wanting the other boy to understand that he wasn't afraid of him. Then he nodded. "Okay," he agreed. It was what they had been doing all week.

"I don't understand it," Ashley complained again. She shook her head. "I guess I'd better take it apart again after school."

T'Ara nodded solemnly. "I will help," she offered.

Riv just rolled his eyes in disgust. But he did tell Jake what he wanted for his lunch, and then ate it ravenously when Jake and Nog returned with the food. He was still getting used to eating regular meals, that much was clear.

The rest of the classes went fairly smoothly, mostly because Riv tried hard to look as if he were sleeping through them. Ms. O'Brien refused to be baited and continued as if he were paying complete attention. Jake wasn't sure it was having any effect on Riv, but at least it helped everyone else.

After lessons were finished, Riv "suddenly" woke up and shot out of the door. Ashley and T'Ara headed for the replicator, ready to get back to work. Jake and Nog wandered together back to the Promenade.

"So," Jake asked his Ferengi friend, "what do you think of Riv?"

"Nothing," Nog replied. "I have no intention of thinking about him at all. I'm too busy thinking about that freighter we saw earlier."

"He seems very unhappy," Jake continued. "Do you think he'll get used to life here?"

Nog shrugged. "He'd better. Who cares?" He grinned. "Let's talk about *important* things. Like money."

"Nog, this *is* important," replied Jake.

"Humans," muttered Nog. He made it sound like an insult. "Look, Riv's uncle works for my uncle in the bar. I've met the man—he's a fat, lazy thing, with all the personality of a dead fish. No wonder Riv doesn't like the guy. Nobody else does, either. So I think Riv's problems are his own; *my* problem is getting some money. Why don't you concentrate on that?"

Jake sighed. It was obvious that Nog wasn't interested. He wasn't sure why he should care about the Bajoran boy, either, but he couldn't help feeling sorry for Riv. He'd had a rough life, and now he was stuck here. Maybe there was something he could do to help him—but what?

Ashley bit at her lower lip, concentrating hard on the computer chip board she was examining. A wisp of her blond hair fell into her eyes. She brushed it back, not even noticing the dark, oily streak her fingers left on her skin. Something was definitely very odd here.

"You have found the problem?" asked T'Ara, raising a pointy eyebrow.

"I think so," Ashley replied. "I checked out this chip yesterday. It's part of the command code mechanism. There was a small cross-circuit between these two points. I removed it, and that should have fixed things."

T'Ara peered down at the board. The gleam of metal where Ashley was pointing was quite obvious. "It appears that the cross-circuit is still there," she commented.

"Not *still there,*" answered Ashley. *"Back* again." She tapped the board in her palm. "You know what it looks like to me? I think somebody's *deliberately* sabotaging my repairs."

Raising her eyebrow again, T'Ara asked, "You are sure?"

"It's the only answer that makes sense," Ashley told her. "I've been trying to find a broken part or some other problem. I thought it was just the equipment breaking

down as usual. But *this* isn't an accident. Somebody had to have deliberately put it there, because I *know* I took it out yesterday."

The Vulcan girl frowned slightly. "But who would do a thing like that?" she objected. "And why?"

"I don't know," Ashley admitted. "But when I *do* find out, whoever it is will pay for trying to make me look bad. I can promise you that. He or she is gonna regret this."

CHAPTER 3

Jake stopped by the living quarters he shared with his father. Despite the fact that Commander Benjamin Sisko was in charge of Deep Space Nine, their rooms on the station were smaller than the ones they'd shared in other places. Jake couldn't really think of them as "home"—they were just rooms to sleep in, to study in, and to store things in. He glanced at the computer pad and saw that his father was going to be on duty for another hour or so, which meant Jake had some free time.

He glanced at the baseball and catcher's mitt on his table. A game on the holodeck? No, he didn't really feel like it right now. Maybe after dinner. At the moment there was just one thing on his mind: Riv Jakar. He still felt sorry for the boy and wondered what he could do to make the Bajoran more at home on DS9. Home! Jake shook his head. *He* didn't feel like this was really home, so how could he help Riv? After all, Commander Sisko had been posted to four starships and two planetary bases that Jake could remember. It was always possible that any day now Starfleet would move him again, and Jake would have to go with his father, leaving behind all his friends on the station.

Riv, on the other hand, looked as if he was stuck here whether he liked it or not. Jake made up his mind to head over to Quark's place. Nog would be there, so he'd at least have someone to talk to, and maybe he'd run into Riv as well. Whether that would be a good or bad thing, Jake couldn't say.

In the center of Deep Space Nine was the Promenade. It was kind of like a shopping center in space. Nog's uncle, Quark, owned a large part of the place. Quark's was a bar, a gambling salon, and a whole mess of holosuites. Visitors and staff could eat, drink, and play there, and they often spent a lot of money. Like all Ferengi, Quark loved making money.

The place was busy, as always, when Jake arrived. He spotted Nog at about the same time that the Ferengi boy spotted him. Jake asked him: "Which one is Riv's uncle?"

Nog grimaced. "Back to that, are you? I don't know why you even think about that horrible brat."

Jake couldn't resist a grin. "That's what everyone said to me when I made friends with you."

"It's not the same thing at all," Nog complained. Then he pointed. "That's him, over there—the one that looks like one of those Earth creatures we studied in class. You know, a walrus."

Riv's uncle was working at one of the game tables, and Jake could see why Nog had called him a walrus. The

19

Bajoran man was very large and tubby, and beneath his ridged Bajoran nose he had a large, prickly-looking mustache that stuck out several inches on either side. With his dark hair and small eyes, the man did look like a walrus on a beach. The scowl on his face didn't look encouraging, either.

"He doesn't look too friendly," Jake said.

"He isn't," said Nog, scowling. "I can see why Riv has problems with him."

"That's only one reason," said Riv. Jake whirled around, unaware that the Bajoran boy had managed to sneak up behind him.

"You startled me!" he said. "I didn't hear you coming."

"I was in the Bajoran underground," Riv reminded him. "You learn to be quiet. If you're not, you get to be dead very quickly. Satisfied yet? Or are you gonna sneak about some more and pry into my private life?"

Jake felt his face get hot. "I was just trying to help," he muttered.

"Well, *don't!*" snarled Riv. "I've had all the help I can take! If it weren't for interfering do-gooders, I'd still be back on Bajor. Instead, I'm stuck on this dump of a space station with a bunch of jerks in some dumb class and living with an uncle who hates me. *Now* do you get why I don't like it here?"

Nodding, Jake said: "Yes, I guess it would be hard for things to get much worse for you, wouldn't it?" He smiled. "So why not make things a bit better instead? Nog and I would like you to come to the Arcade with us." He gave his Ferengi friend a kick. "Wouldn't we?"

"Oh, sure," said Nog without any enthusiasm. "I just love hanging out with antisocial parasites with attitude problems."

Talk about no help at all . . . "He's just joking," Jake told Riv, hoping the Bajoran would believe it.

"Right. I've heard a lot about the Ferengi sense of humor." He gave a nasty little smile. "They say you have to cut a Ferengi into *very* little pieces to find it."

This was obviously not working out. "Look," said Jake, sighing, "the offer's open. Any time you want a friend, I'll be around. Till then—" He stopped talking, realizing that Riv wasn't listening. The Bajoran's eyes had narrowed to slits, and he was hissing softly as he stared past Jake and Nog. Puzzled, Jake turned around to see what had caught Riv's attention.

It was Garak, the tailor. He was the only Cardassian who had remained behind when the army of occupation had left Deep Space Nine. Like all Cardassians, Garak was tall and skinny. His long neck ended in a vaguely reptilian face, gray in color, and with just the hint of scales. Despite his ferocious appearance, he had deep eyes that held more than a sparkle of humor in them. Jake had met him only once, but there was something rather likable about him.

"There are still *Cardassians* on this station?" whispered Riv, his mouth twitching angrily at the edges. "You didn't kill them all off?"

"We didn't kill *any* of them," Jake replied. "The war's over, remember? They all left, except Garak. He owns the clothing store on the Promenade."

"It's easy for you to say the war's over," Riv said

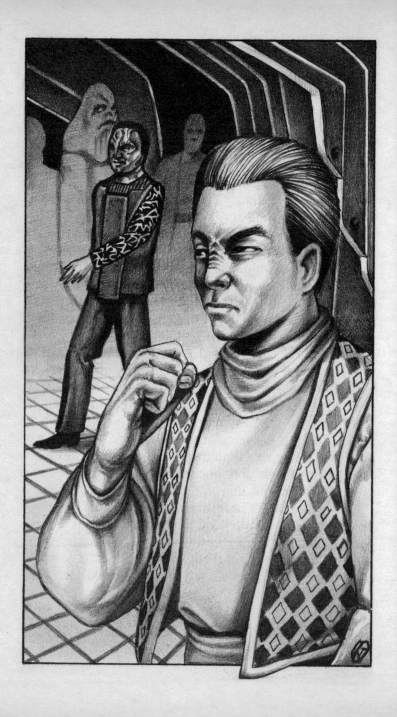

angrily. *"Your* parents weren't murdered by the Cardassians. That one should be thrown out of the nearest airlock to breath space."

"Garak's okay," replied Jake. "He's not a soldier, he's a shopkeeper."

"All Cardassians are alike," snapped Riv. "Killers. It's them or us." His eyes narrowed again. "And I'm gonna fix that one."

Jake didn't like the sound of that threat. Riv seemed to be the sort of person who carried things through. "Don't do anything stupid," he warned.

"Stupid is letting one of those monsters on the station," Riv growled. Then he stormed off.

After a moment's silence Nog grinned. "Well, I think you've shown that Riv really *is* as bad as his uncle claims. Now can we do something interesting? There's gotta be a way for me to make some money, if I can just figure out what. . . ."

Jake wasn't really paying attention. Did Riv *really* mean to do something about Garak? If so—what? Should he tell his father so that Riv could be watched? Or was that what Riv wanted? If he *did* tell his father, then there was no chance that Riv would ever come to accept him as a friend. He sighed. Whatever he did was likely to be wrong. But in a situation like this, how could he decide what to do?

The following morning Jake, Ashley, and T'Ara arrived in class almost together. "Did you get the replicator fixed?" he asked them.

"Yeah," Ashley told him. "But we made a real interesting discovery. *Somebody* fixed the machine so that it only made stew and cheesecake."

"But who'd do a thing like that?" asked Jake, puzzled.

"We have not been able to discover the answer as yet," T'Ara replied. "But Ashley has come up with a possible way to resolve the problem."

"Way to go," said Jake, approvingly. Before he could ask more questions, Ms. O'Brien entered the class. Nog followed and slid into his seat. The two girls sat down as well. As they all switched on their computers, Riv sauntered in, hands in his pockets and looking bored. Jake was quite surprised that the Bajoran boy had bothered to come to class, but nodded to him. Riv ignored him but sat down at the desk he had occupied the previous day.

"Right," Ms. O'Brien said. "Today, let's study a little history. Who can tell me who invented warp drive?"

Ashley's hand shot up. "Zephram Cochrane," she announced. "In the year 2061." She grinned. "Easy. In fact—"

She broke off as the door hissed open. Into the room strode two adults. One of them was Garak, the Cardassian tailor, looking rather unhappy. The other was Odo.

Odo was nice enough, but there was something very spooky about him. He was the station's constable, in charge of law and order. He always wore a brown uniform and a very severe expression. He looked human enough, in a sort of unfinished way. There weren't any lines on his face, for example, and his ears didn't look quite right. His hair looked like it was a wig, and his eyes

24

seemed to be a bit too deeply set. The reason was simple: This was as close to human as Odo could get. He wasn't actually what he appeared to be. In his natural state he looked like a pool of jelly. But he was able to change his shape into anything he liked, just by concentrating on it.

He always looked grim. Jake supposed that being the policeman on the station wasn't exactly the sort of job to bring a smile to anyone's face. Odo looked as if he'd never even learned *how* to smile—and that was on his good days. Right now he was looking ferocious enough to curdle milk with one glance.

"Excuse me," he said politely but firmly to Ms. O'Brien. "But I need to have a few words with your class."

"Of course." The teacher looked puzzled. "Is there something wrong, Odo?"

"Yes." His eyes scanned the room and the silent students. "It appears that we have a thief in here." His eyes fastened directly on Nog.

CHAPTER 4

Why are you looking at me?" demanded Nog defensively. "I've done nothing wrong!"

"Did I say you had?" asked Odo. "Perhaps you have a guilty conscience?" Before Nog could reply, Odo held up his hand. "Garak came to me this morning with a complaint, and I am investigating it. It seems that someone has stolen several items of clothing from his store."

"I didn't see who did it," Garak put in, wringing his hands together uncomfortably. "Just a small shape in the darkness. By the time that I put on the shop lights, whoever it was had vanished."

"If there *was* anybody," Riv said, sneering. "We only have his word for it—and I'd trust a Cardassian about as far as I could spit one."

Odo eyed the Bajoran boy. "Ah, yes—Riv Jakar, isn't it? I've heard a lot about you. None of it good."

"And I've heard a lot about you, too," Riv replied. "You worked with the Cardassians while they ran this station, didn't you? And now you're helping one of the monsters to frame us for theft."

"My job is to keep the peace and enforce justice," Odo answered. "It doesn't matter *who* is in charge of the station—*I* guarantee justice. And I didn't simply take Garak's word for his losses. I checked his computer logs, and the items *are* missing. Clothing for a girl—stolen by a small thief."

"Don't look at me!" protested Nog. "Hey! You said it was girl's clothing that was stolen! Maybe one of *them* did it!" He pointed vaguely across the room.

"Gee, thanks a lot," said Ashley sarcastically. "You think *I'd* go stealing clothes? No way!"

"And Vulcans do not steal," added T'Ara, looking slightly smug, despite her supposed lack of emotions.

"Nor do they lie," agreed Odo. Then he glared down at her. "But if a Vulcan were capable of one, then she could do the other, couldn't she?" Without waiting for a reply, he turned to Marn Laren. "What about you?" he asked.

"What about me?" she replied, scowling hard. "You think *I* stole from that Cardassian? I wouldn't be caught dead touching his things."

Odo shook his head. "Well, I didn't expect a confession from the thief. But whoever it was, I promise you that person will be caught. And punished." He looked slowly about the room again. "So be warned. If there is another incident, I shall be *very* annoyed." With a curt nod to Ms. O'Brien, he marched out of the room. Garak gave a helpless shrug and followed him out.

As soon as the door closed, Riv muttered, "I still think

he's lying. It's the Cardassian national sport. He's just trying to get us into trouble."

"Why would he want to do that?" asked Jake, puzzled.

"Because he's a *Cardassian,* you idiot," snapped Riv. "They just love to cause trouble."

"Then you must be a Cardassian in disguise," Ashley said coldly. "Because that's all *you* seem to do."

Riv went pale: "Take that back," he snarled. "Or I'll break your neck."

"Yeah?" Ashley wrinkled her nose. "I'm not scared of you."

"That's quite enough!" Ms. O'Brien broke in calmly but firmly. "Ashley, there is no need to trade insults with Riv. And there's no need for you to start a fight, Riv. You have to learn to get along with other people. Even Cardassians," she added.

"Oh, I get along with Cardassians," Riv replied, settling down. He gave a smirk. *"Dead* ones. And I'll fix that lying tailor, you wait and see."

"Well," the teacher said, "right now you're going to get back to your lessons—all of you."

Jake's eyes returned to his computer screen, but his mind was still focused on Riv. There had been a look in the other boy's eyes that seemed to say he meant business. Jake was convinced that Riv had already come up with an idea for getting back at Garak. His hatred of the Cardassians was not wearing away. If anything, it seemed to be getting stronger. And he appeared to have chosen Garak to suffer his anger.

Then there was this stealing thing. He didn't like

thinking that Nog was guilty, but . . . well, Nog *could* be guilty. He'd been talking about making money all last night. Or Riv could have done it, to strike back at a Cardassian. Still, why would either of them steal girl's clothes? The more he thought about it, the more certain he became that Riv wouldn't have done anything so minor. And as for Nog—*he* wanted to make money. If he had stolen the clothes, who could he possibly sell them to that wouldn't know they were stolen? It didn't make much sense. And he couldn't imagine that any of the girls in the class would have done it. Ashley had the skill to bypass the alarms, but she wasn't the sort of person who'd steal anything. As for T'Ara—*she* never did anything without a very good, logical reason. Marn disliked Garak too much to even approach his shop. And the other girls were really too young even to think about stealing anything from anywhere.

Eventually it was lunch break. Ms. O'Brien stared at the replicator rather nervously. "You *did* fix this thing, Ashley?" she asked.

"Oh, yes," Ashley assured her. "T'Ara and I both did it."

"Then it will work this time?" asked the teacher.

"I doubt it," said Ashley cheerfully. "Unless you're into stew and cheesecake." She crossed over to the replicator before Ms. O'Brien could ask her what she meant. "Blueberry pie and chocolate ice cream," she ordered.

There was a moment's pause, and then a dish slowly materialized inside the chamber. Jake stared at it. Hot,

steaming stew, with a slice of cheesecake melting into it. . . .

Strangely enough, Ashley didn't seem at all upset. Instead, she wrenched off the access panel at the side of the machine. With a probe, she snapped out one of the chip boards. "Just as I thought," she said happily. She pointed to a small piece of wire wrapped across the contacts.

"But you removed that wire last night," T'Ara said, struggling to keep her face straight.

"And somebody put it back," Ashley finished. "This *proves* that the problems with the replicator aren't an accident."

"Pretty neat," Jake said. "But it doesn't help us find out *who* did it."

"Yes it does," said Ashley smugly. "You see, when I was sure the unit was being sabotaged, I set up a program. Whoever rewired this chip had to have touched it. I set it to scan the culprit." She pulled a small tricorder from her belt. "I've accessed the files of everyone on the station, and all I have to do is cross-check them against the readings from this chip, and we'll know who's the stew-and-cheesecake maniac."

"Clever," Jake admitted, impressed with her thinking.

"I know I am," agreed Ashley. She plugged the chip into the tricorder and hit the button to start the check. A moment later she frowned. "That's odd."

"What's wrong?" asked Riv, smirking. "Screwed up, have you? Maybe you're not as clever as you think you are."

Ignoring this taunt, Ashley stared at the screen of the tricorder in disbelief. "There's no match at all."

Nog shrugged. "Maybe the chip didn't get a sample, then?" he suggested.

"No, there's definitely a sample," Ashley said. She shook her head. "But the computer can't match it against any of the files."

"Maybe," said Marn, "that's because the files haven't

been updated for a little while." She glared at Riv. "I'll bet *he's* not in them yet."

Riv gave her a cold look. "Are you accusing *me* of fixing the machine?" he asked. "Why would I bother?"

"Besides," added Jake, "the replicator wasn't working before Riv arrived on the station."

"But we don't know that it was sabotaged back then," Marn continued. "It may have been a genuine error before. And we've all seen how good Riv is with computers."

"How would you like to see how good I am with my fists?" Riv snapped.

Ms. O'Brien moved between them. "That's quite enough," she said firmly. "I want you all to cool off. Meanwhile," she added with a sigh, "it looks like we'll be bringing lunch in again."

After school was over, Jake pulled Nog aside. "Riv's up to something," he said. "I just don't know what. Did you see his reaction to Garak?"

"Who cares?" asked Nog. "It's either Ms. O'Brien's or Odo's problem, not ours. We should mind our own business. There's no profit in minding theirs."

"It could be something that would affect us," Jake said. "He seems to have a grudge against us all. He could get us all into trouble."

Nog was uncertain. "You're just guessing," he complained.

"But it's a good guess." Jake saw that he had his friend worried enough to act. "Look, let's just keep our eyes open and see what he's up to, okay? Nothing more than that."

"Well, okay," agreed Nog finally. He went along with Jake to the Promenade. "As long as it doesn't take too much time."

"Riv's not very patient," Jake pointed out. "Whatever he's planning, he's bound to do it soon." He just wished he had some idea what it might be.

"Okay," said Ashley when she was alone in the classroom with T'Ara. "My last plan didn't work." She grinned. "Time for Plan B."

"And what is Plan B?" asked T'Ara.

Ashley showed her the computer chip pad. "I've removed the wire again, and this time I've added a small transmitter. When our culprit puts the wire back, it'll sent a signal out." She snapped the chip back into the replicator and closed the cover. "I've got my notepad computer set to warn me when that happens. All we have to do is to hang around until the alarm goes off. Then we jump whoever it is."

T'Ara nodded solemnly. "It is a good plan," she agreed. "And when we catch the culprit?"

"We turn him in to Odo," Ashley said. "But first . . ." She gave a broad smile. "I'm going to make one last batch of stew and cheesecake—and rub his face in it!"

CHAPTER 5

This is really boring," Nog said. He was sitting on the Upper Level of the Promenade, his feet hanging down, kicking them back and forth. His chin was pressed against the restraint bar that kept him from falling to the Main Level twenty feet below.

"You've said that seven times now," Jake complained. He was sitting next to Nog and feeling just as bored himself.

"That's because it's *really* boring," Nog grumbled. "We've been here all evening, wasting our time watching Riv do nothing. We could have been making money, but no, *you* decided we have to watch that boring Bajoran. Now all the stores are closing, and we've got nothing to show for the whole time."

"Riv's up to something," insisted Jake.

"Yeah," agreed Nog. "He's trying to bore us to death! Let's just give up and go home."

"No," said Jake stubbornly. "He's going to do something. I *know* it." As he spoke, he grabbed Nog's

shoulder and pointed. "Look, there he is! He's crossing the Promenade."

There were only a dozen or so people moving about now, and it wasn't hard to see the small Bajoran figure. Nog frowned. "So? He's probably gonna buy another frozen *yashi* treat." He licked his lips at the thought. "And it's not a bad idea."

"The booth is closed," Jake answered. "Anyway, he's sticking to the shadows."

Riv was walking slowly and darting quick glances around. As Jake watched, he realized that the Bajoran boy had a small bundle of cloth in his hands.

"Look," he said softly. "He's carrying something. And he's making for Garak's shop." An idea hit him. "Maybe that's a bundle of the stolen clothing, and he's aiming to put them back?"

"It's a bit late now," Nog objected. "They've already been reported as stolen."

"Well, maybe he wants Garak to look stupid, then?" suggested Jake. "Like the stuff wasn't stolen after all." He rose to his feet. "Let's follow him."

Nog considered Jake's suggestion as he followed his friend. He shook his head. "Odo would never fall for it," he said in a quiet voice. "He checked the computer records, remember."

"Yeah, *we* know Odo wouldn't be taken in," agreed Jake. He winced at the memory of a couple of pranks he and Nog had pulled that had brought Odo's wrath down on them. "But Riv isn't as smart as we are, is he?"

"Nobody's as smart as we are," Nog replied. Then he grimaced. "Except maybe Odo."

Jake stopped Nog, and they hugged the wall. The Promenade was now empty, except for the two of them and Riv. The Bajoran boy had reached Garak's closed shop, and he glanced around. When he saw nothing to alarm him, he tapped something into the small computer screen by the shop. The door hissed softly open, and Riv slid inside.

"He's overridden the security codes," said Nog. There was admiration in his voice. "I wonder if he'll teach me that trick?"

"Come on," Jake instructed. He led the way softly across the Promenade. They halted beside the open door, and Jake took a quick glance inside the shop. There was a nightlight inside that burned low. It gave just enough illumination to show the racks of clothing as shadows. He could see Riv at the far side of the room, close to the counter. With a jerk of his head Jake indicated to Nog that they should slip inside the store. Jake moved quickly and quietly, then crouched behind a rack of clothes. Through the gaps he saw Nog take up a similar position behind a different rack. Together they watched Riv.

The Bajoran boy was unwrapping the bundle he'd been carrying. In the low light it was hard for Jake to see what Riv was doing, but it looked as if he had a small machine or something he was tinkering with.

There was the click of a switch, then Riv jumped to his feet. With a wide grin on his face, he hurried back toward the entrance. He passed by Jake and Nog, who were virtually invisible in their hiding places. Riv paused long enough to tap another command into the security pad by the door, and then hurried off as the door hissed closed again.

Now that they were alone, Jake moved out into the aisle. Nog joined him and they both stared at the counter. In front of it was the cloak Riv had been carrying, and in the folds of the cloak Jake could make out a small box. Even in the dim light the glitter of metal was unmistakable.

"What could that be?" asked Jake.

"Let's find out," said Nog, grinning. He scuttled forward and bent over the device. As Jake joined him, Nog almost jumped out of his skin. "It's a bomb!" he exclaimed.

Jake's pulse raced. "A bomb?" he asked nervously. "Are you sure?"

"Yeah." Nog pointed at the small box. There was a flat, dull package attached, and a contact running from it to a small, round dial on the box. "That's vebrite—a Bajoran explosive. It's not very powerful, but it burns like crazy. I *definitely* think it's time we were out of here!"

Jake grabbed him before he could scamper away. Standing this close to the bomb made him sick in his stomach, but he couldn't just run away. "We can't just leave it to explode," he said.

"Can't we?" asked Nog. "You just watch."

Jake wouldn't let go, despite Nog's struggles. "It must be safe for a few more minutes," he argued. "Riv would have set it to give himself time." He stared at the small dial. It was a clock of some kind, calibrated in Bajoran time. He did a rough calculation. "We've got loads of time—at least five minutes."

"Great," said Nog. "We can be back in my uncle's place when it goes off."

"We should call Odo," Jake argued.

"You call Odo. I'll see you tomorrow."

Jake had an idea. He let go of his grip on Nog. "Okay, off you go." He managed a small smile, despite the sickly twitching in his stomach. "Riv locked the door as he left. You think you can override it in less than five minutes?"

The thought obviously hadn't occurred to Nog. The small Ferengi froze, and his face went even paler. "Uh . . . no." He chewed at his lip thoughtfully. "You got a better idea?"

Jake wished he had one of the small communicator badges that his father and the other Starfleet officers wore. "Is there a communicator or something in the store we could use to call for help?"

Nog shrugged. "How should I know? I don't come in here much. I *hate* buying clothes."

It was a feeling Jake shared—and wished he didn't. There probably was a communicator somewhere in Garak's shop, but where? "Maybe we could smash a window?" he suggested. "That's bound to bring Odo or one of his officers. And we could get out of the hole."

"No use," said Nog with a sigh. "They replaced all the windows with shatterproof plasteel in the riots after the Cardassians left. The shopkeepers got tired of sweeping up all the mess. Nothing short of a phaser will break the windows now."

There was a terrible pain in Jake's stomach. He knew it was fear. Being trapped inside a store with a ticking bomb was definitely not high on a list of his favorite activities. "Uh . . . I'm open to suggestions," he said.

"Oh, right," muttered Nog. "Get me into this and expect me to get us out." He rolled his eyes. "Okay, you take a look for a communicator. I'll see if I can do anything with the bomb."

"You mean like trying to *defuse* it?" asked Jake, shocked.

Nog scowled. "You think I'd try to *explode* it?" he snapped. "Of course I mean try to defuse it."

"Are you sure you know what you're doing?" asked Jake very nervously.

"Ask me again in just over four minutes," Nog suggested. "If we're gonna get killed anyway, what difference does it make? So start looking, okay?"

Jake didn't reply; he couldn't think of anything to say. In four minutes they might both be dead. . . . He swallowed hard and watched Nog kneel next to the bomb. He really hoped that his friend did have some idea of what he was doing. Almost anything could go wrong and set the bomb off early. The best thing he could do was to find a communicator—fast!

He could feel himself sweating uncomfortably as he moved to the counter and started to search the drawers there. He found plenty of small measuring devices, size charts, and style books. There were computer disks and even antiques like scissors. But there was no sign of a communicator.

Nervously wondering how long there was left, he moved across to a small storage alcove. Jake started to search the alcove. Once again, there were plenty of supplies, but no sign of a communicator. There couldn't be much time left now. . . . He used a spare piece of cloth to wipe the sweat from his brow and then glanced at Nog. His Ferengi friend had managed to take part of the clock apart, and there were several small pieces scattered on the floor now. From the mutterings he could hear, though, it sounded as if Nog hadn't disarmed the device yet. Now what?

His eyes fell on one of the tools he'd found. A laser cutter, used by Garak to rough-cut the clothes he made. He picked it up and clicked the switch on. The beam that was produced was faint and feeble, but it was better than nothing. It was only meant for cutting cloth and such, but maybe he could use it to cut through the lock on the door so they could escape. He opened his mouth to tell Nog, then decided against it.

Slipping past his friend, he rushed to the door, clutching the cutter. He switched it on again and held it against the lock. It was hard to see if he was having any effect for several long, frightening seconds. Then he saw a faint glow in the door, and a drop of metal dripped free.

It was working! But would it be in time? He darted another look at the bomb. He wished he could ask how long they had left, but he didn't dare distract Nog. Instead, he concentrated on the lock. Another gleaming drop of metal trickled down the doorway.

It was going to take too long. . . .

"Uh-oh," said Nog.

Jake's stomach did a backflip. "What do you mean *uh-oh?*" he almost yelled.

"I mean we've got about five seconds left on the clock." Nog jumped to his feet and ran to join Jake at the door. "I *think* I managed to stop the detonator. But I'm not sure."

"Be sure!" Jake yelled as Nog tried to hide behind him.

There was a very loud click from the bomb.

Then nothing.

Nog peered out from under Jake's arm. "I'm sure," he finally said.

"You did it!" exclaimed Jake. "You stopped the bomb."

"Yeah," agreed Nog. Jake would have been happier if Nog had looked less surprised. "I'm an expert at scavenging," he explained. "I learned it when the Cardassians were here. I guess you never forget stuff like that." He grinned, showing all his pointy teeth. "Hey, maybe I could sell that vebrite?" he said. "It's pretty valuable stuff." He went back to the littered remains of the bomb and started to scoop them up in the cloak.

Jake returned to work on the lock. The urgency was gone now, but they still had to get out. Finally there was a dull *snick,* and the door gave slightly. "I've done it," he called to Nog. "Come on, let's get out of here."

"You don't need to tell me twice," Nog muttered. He had all the pieces of the bomb wrapped back up in the cloak, which he tucked under his arm. "Let's go."

Jake slid the door open, and they almost jumped out

of the store. Jake slid the door closed behind them, and they turned to flee.

Facing them was Odo, and he had his sternest expression on his face.

"Well," he growled, "what have we here? Late-night shoppers, I assume. Let me have a look at that," he added, pointing at the cloak Nog was clutching.

"You're not going to like it," Nog warned him.

"I'll be the judge of that," Odo snapped. "Let me see."

Reluctantly Nog opened up the bundle. Odo's eyes opened wide.

"A vebrite bomb?" he said in shock.

"I told you you weren't gonna like it," Nog muttered.

Jake winced. He almost wished the bomb had gone off. It was quite clear from the grim expression written on Odo's face that he and Nog were in very serious trouble this time.

CHAPTER 6

Ashley stared at her computer pad for something like the sixtieth time. Still no sign that anyone had tried to tamper with the replicator. As she looked up, she saw T'Ara try to hide a yawn and felt guilty. T'Ara acted much older than her age, and Ashley often forgot that she was only seven. "I'm sorry," she said. "It's kind of late, isn't it, and you must be really bored."

T'Ara managed to raise her right eyebrow in the Vulcan equivalent of a puzzled expression. "Boredom is an emotion," she replied. "And Vulcans do not have emotions."

This wasn't really true, and Ashley knew it. T'Ara *did* have emotions, but Vulcans weren't supposed to let them take control of their lives, so they buried them. Though she was pretty good at it, T'Ara wasn't perfect. Ashley wondered if most Vulcans ever were completely in control of all of their emotions, whatever they claimed.

"Well, it's still late," she said. "And *I'm* bored. It's been a complete waste of time, hasn't it?"

"It has been rather . . . uneventful," agreed T'Ara. It was probably as close as she could come to admitting she was totally bored. "It might be best to—"

The alarm on Ashley's pad suddenly beeped several times very rapidly. Even T'Ara looked startled for a second before she could wipe the shock off her face.

"There's someone at the replicator!" Ashley said, grinning. She hadn't screwed up, after all! "All right!" The two girls clambered to their feet and moved quietly down the corridor toward the schoolroom. They had deliberately hidden in an adjoining corridor so that any intruder wouldn't see them. Outside the schoolroom they both stopped. There was a small glass panel in the wall next to the door. Even with the lights on low to save power during the night, it was possible to see some details inside the room. T'Ara, being several inches shorter, had to stand on tiptoes, but together she and Ashley peered into the room.

The place was still and dark. At first only the black shapes of the desks were visible. Then Ashley gave a soft exclamation. Beside the small replicator she could just make out a shadowy figure.

"Shall we go in?" asked T'Ara in a whisper.

"Not yet," Ashley replied. "I want to see who it is first. When he or she turns around, we should be able to spot them. You wanna bet it's that Riv?"

"Vulcans do not gamble," T'Ara answered, somewhat smugly. "And certainly not on such a bad bet as that."

"Chicken," muttered Ashley. She held her breath as the shadowy figure inside the room put the replicator cover back in place. When the mysterious saboteur turned around, Ashley couldn't stop herself gasping in shock.

It was obvious that the saboteur wasn't Riv. Nor was it anyone else in their class. In the pale light the gray and scaly skin was quite clear, as was the long knot of dark hair that ran down the young girl's back.

"It is a *Cardassian* girl!" exclaimed T'Ara—in her shock completely forgetting her claim to not have emotions. "But . . . how?"

"Stay still!" hissed Ashley furiously. All her plans had collapsed with this revelation. She'd been expecting Riv—and, if not him, then someone else that they knew. Ashley had then intended to open the door and switch on the lights, catching the culprit in the act. But this revelation had shattered her ideas. Cardassians were very quick and very nasty when they wanted to be. Whoever this girl was, she had to be here illegally. If Ashley opened the door and surprised her, then the girl might be desperate enough to attack them.

If she were on her own, Ashley might have risked it. The Cardassian was tall and thin, but she didn't look any older or stronger than she was. But there was T'Ara to think about.

The Cardassian was looking around the schoolroom. Ashley froze. Could the girl inside see them at the window, despite the low level of lighting? She didn't know how good Cardassian eyes were. After a moment, though, the girl seemed satisfied. She tapped in a command on the replicator board. There was a sparkle of light, and the now-familiar shape of a bowl of stew and cheesecake appeared. The girl picked it up and then

47

hurried to the side wall. Ashley hadn't been looking in that direction before, but she now saw a thin, metallic rope hanging from a gap in the ceiling of the room. With astonishing speed the Cardassian climbed this rope. A moment later it was jerked out of sight. Then the dark shape of the hole also vanished as the girl obviously replaced the ceiling tile she'd slid aside earlier.

Ashley let her breath out in one long gasp. "So *that's* who's been sabotaging my repairs," she muttered. "A Cardassian, hiding out in the ceiling."

"But—why?" asked T'Ara. She'd finally managed to get her face under control again, and she looked as blank as usual. "I do not understand."

"Nor do I," admitted Ashley. "But I think we should take a look, don't you?"

"Now?" T'Ara sounded a little worried.

"No," Ashley replied. "In the morning. I'll bet she sleeps in the daytime and comes out like that at night when she's on her own." She snapped her fingers. "Of course! There was that Cardassian freighter that docked here a week or so back! I'll bet she came here on that and has been hiding out ever since."

"It is logical," agreed T'Ara. "But not sensible. Why should she do that?"

"We'll find out when we talk to her tomorrow." Ashley smiled grimly. "We'll get Jake and Nog in on this, too. They'll be surprised—and impressed with what we've discovered! I'll call Jake now and get him to meet us before school starts so we can catch that girl." She tapped his room number on the pad, but there was no reply.

"You think he has gone to bed?" asked T'Ara.

"No way," Ashley said firmly. "He *hates* going to bed early." She glanced around and saw one of the computer terminals in a nearby wall. She hurried over to it and slapped the panel. "Computer, where's Jake Sisko?"

The panel lit up. In a pleasant voice the computer replied: "He is in Odo's office."

"Odo's office?" repeated Ashley, puzzled. "What's he doing there?" She hadn't meant this as a question for the computer to answer, but the computer didn't know that.

"He is being questioned about a bomb," the computer said.

"A bomb?" T'Ara couldn't keep the astonishment out of her voice. "What's he doing with a *bomb?*"

"What are you doing with a bomb?" asked Commander Sisko, obviously trying hard to keep his temper under control.

Jake felt miserable. He liked his father a whole lot; they were best of friends, most of the time. But his father was in charge of Deep Space Nine, and Jake knew he wouldn't let anything or anyone—not even his son—endanger the station. But he just didn't know what he could say in reply. It was bad enough facing Odo's firm but insistent questioning. Answering his father was even worse.

"Uh . . . we found it," he finally said. He realized how lame that was.

"You *found* it?" his father repeated. "You tripped over it on your way home, you mean?" His eyes were almost blazing with anger.

49

"Well," Odo said carefully, "they *might* have . . . *if* their way home happened to be through Garak's locked store." He tapped the laser cutter in his hand.

Commander Sisko turned to glare down at Nog. "What were you two doing in Garak's store?" he asked.

"Finding a bomb?" Nog answered hopefully.

"I see." His father turned back to Jake. "And did you just run into it purely by chance, or did you happen to know it was there?"

"Well," Jake admitted, "we didn't exactly know *it* was there. But we did know that *something* was. When we investigated, we found it was a bomb."

"That's right," Nog agreed quickly. "And we were just being good citizens and bringing it over to give to Odo when he found us."

"I see," Commander Sisko said again. "And did you happen to see who it was who was careless enough to leave this bomb lying around for you to trip over?"

"Yes," said Nog.

"No," said Jake quickly. He glared at Nog. "We can't just *tell* them who it was," he hissed.

The Ferengi boy looked puzzled for a moment. Then a wide grin spread over his face. "Smart thinking!" He turned to Jake's father. "We saw who did it—but it'll cost you to find out."

Jake groaned. Nog picked the wrong times to try and make money. "That's not what I meant! You can't *sell* your friends!"

"You can sell *anything* if you know how," Nog replied. "Besides, the person who planted the bomb isn't our friend. He said so, remember?"

Commander Sisko broke in. "Let me get this straight," he said, ice dripping from his voice. "You saw who did it but you want to be *paid* to tell us?"

"Yes," said Nog.

"No," Jake insisted. Nog scowled at him, but Jake ignored it. "Look," he said to his father, trying to get him to understand, "I don't think telling on him will help."

His father glanced down at the remains of the bomb. "Help him or help us?" He shook his head. "Jake, I don't understand you in this. Whoever planted this bomb has no regard for property or life. You *must* tell us who it was."

Jake was well and truly caught now. If he told them about Riv, then the Bajoran boy would be convinced that everyone hated him. It would only make him worse. On the other hand, he couldn't let his father down, nor allow Riv to come up with more plans that might be even more dangerous the next time. "I need to think about it some more," he finally replied.

"Take as long as you like," Odo suggested. "I've already sent one of my deputies out to bring in the person responsible." At the surprised expression on Jake's face he almost cracked a smile. "It's not hard to deduce who could have made that bomb, and who's been having problems ever since he arrived on this station." As he spoke, the door hissed open.

The deputy saluted and escorted in Riv and his uncle Bothna. The tubby man appeared to have been woken up from a sound sleep. He was grouchy and untidy, still straightening his clothes.

Riv simply looked part angry, part bored. His eyes fastened on the remains of the bomb and then on Jake and Nog. "So you saw me plant it and ratted on me?" he said. "Well, I can't say I'm surprised."

"We didn't tell them anything about you," Jake answered, his cheeks burning. "Odo guessed it was you."

The constable did smile this time. "And we all just heard you admit it," he added.

Riv shrugged. "Big deal." He gave Jake a curious look. "You *didn't* tell?" He was clearly puzzled.

"He didn't," Commander Sisko said. "And he could have been in very serious trouble."

Scowling, Riv stared at Jake. "I don't want anyone taking the blame for my actions," he said. Turning back to Odo, he crossed his arms. "I planted the bomb in the Cardassian's store," he confessed. "And I'm willing to accept my punishment."

His uncle went pale. "You *what?*" he squeaked.

"Planted this firebomb in Garak's clothing store," Odo explained, tapping the bits and pieces on his desk.

Bothna whirled to face his nephew. "What were you thinking of?" he cried. He was half-panicking and half-furious. The veins in his thick neck were throbbing.

"They're the *enemy!*" Riv yelled back. "And Garak was trying to stir up trouble against me. I know he was."

"The war is over," Odo said firmly. "You have no enemies at the moment. Though, with your attitude, I suspect there'll be no shortage of them soon." He glowered at Riv. "And Garak refused to press charges against anyone over the missing clothing. It was just one outfit, and he felt that nothing would be gained by making a fuss over it." He picked up the wad of explosive. "I wonder how he'll feel when I tell him about this?"

"Well," demanded Bothna, "what are you going to do with this little terrorist? Throw him in jail?"

Commander Sisko shook his head. "I don't think so," he said. "I think the best thing for now is to release him into your custody."

"What?" Bothna went pale again. "But . . . you *have* to lock him up! He's a potential killer!"

"He's a *boy,*" Odo growled. "And you're his uncle— and legal guardian. *You're* responsible for him."

"I don't want anything to do with him," Bothna insisted. "I didn't from the start of this. He's a murderous savage!"

Jake had kept quiet, not wanting to get back into trouble himself, but he couldn't stay silent. "Maybe if you were a bit nicer to him, he wouldn't be so angry all the time," he said.

Bothna glared at him. "Who asked you?" he snapped.

Jake felt his face burning. His father placed an arm about his shoulder and stared back at Bothna. "In this case," he said, "I think Jake is perfectly correct. What that boy needs from you is a little affection and understanding."

"Lock me up!" begged Riv. "I'd rather be in jail than back with *him.*"

Jake's father shook his head. "We can't always get what we'd like," he said with a slight smile on his lips. "Sometimes we have to accept what is best."

Odo stood up and faced Bothna. "Take the boy

home," he growled. "And remember—*you're* responsible for his actions. If he causes any more trouble, it'll be your skin I'll nail to my wall."

"That's not fair!" Bothna wailed.

"No," agreed Odo with another of his rare smiles. "But that won't stop me from enjoying it."

Both Bothna and Riv were obviously in agreement about one thing—probably for the first time in their lives. It was that neither wanted to be with the other. Both of them glared at Odo, then turned and stormed out. When the door closed, Odo turned to face Commander Sisko.

"I'll speak with Garak in the morning about this matter," he said. "I don't know if he'll insist on pressing charges or not. Meanwhile, one of my men is repairing the broken lock." He glared down at Jake. "I don't know whether I owe you my thanks or a good paddling."

"*I* know," his father said in his frostiest voice. "A little of both, probably."

"Hey, we saved the shop," Nog said, wringing his hands. "Doesn't that count for anything?"

"Yes," Commander Sisko agreed. "That's the only thing in your favor at the moment." He looked at Odo. "I'll take these two now," he said. "I'll leave Nog with his father. And then Jake and I are going to have a little chat. . . ."

Jake swallowed hard. He knew he wasn't going to enjoy this conversation. . . .

CHAPTER 7

The following morning when Jake had finished his shower and was getting dressed, he walked warily into the small kitchen of the quarters he and his father shared. Commander Sisko was taking a last sip of coffee before heading off to begin his workday. Jake winced; he'd been delaying, hoping to avoid seeing his father. He was afraid that he'd get another talking to, as he had the previous evening.

His father put down his cup as he headed for the door. "I'm not going to lecture you again, Jake," he said. "I know you did what you felt was best. But please try to *think* in future, and if you have any problems—any problems at all—you should know you can come to me to ask for advice. End of subject—okay?"

"Yeah," agreed Jake, relieved. "I guess I shouldn't have been so secretive and all."

"I said *end of subject*," his father replied, smiling slightly. "And that includes blaming yourself. Enjoy your day at school." He winked and then left the apartment.

Glad that things were back to normal with his father, Jake replicated himself some juice and cereal. He really liked and admired his father, and it had been rough being told off. "Why didn't you just call me or Odo when you saw Riv go into Garak's shop?" his father had demanded. Jake had been forced to admit that he simply hadn't thought of it. He'd been completely intent on watching the Bajoran boy—and had almost been blown up because of it.

As he was swallowing some juice, the flashing Message light on the wall computer caught his eye. Since his father had left, it couldn't be for him. "Computer," he called out, "what's the message?"

"It is from Ashley Fontana," the computer replied. "She asks that you meet her an hour early at school this morning."

An hour early? That was in just a few minutes! He gulped down the rest of his cereal and then washed it down with the last of the juice. After placing the used dishware in the recycler, he grabbed his computer pad and hurried out.

As he approached the classroom, Jake saw that Ashley, T'Ara, and Nog were waiting for him.

"You're late," she told him. "We haven't got much time. Here, hold this." She thrust out a small flashlight, which Jake took automatically.

"Time for what?" he asked, puzzled.

"We have discovered the identity of the person who sabotaged the replicator," T'Ara announced.

"So?" asked Nog. "Who is it?"

Ashley gave a grin as she tapped in the code to open the classroom door. "Nobody we know." As the door opened, she picked up an expandable ladder. "And you'll never guess where this person is hiding."

Jake frowned slightly. Ashley had a ladder and had given him a flashlight. Up, then, and dark . . . "Inside the ceiling?" he guessed.

Ashley wrinkled her nose. "You did guess. Yeah, in the ceiling. Neat, eh?"

"So," Nog repeated impatiently, "who is it?"

"You'll see." Ashley grinned secretively at T'Ara. The Vulcan girl almost smiled back but caught herself just in time. Setting the ladder up close to one wall, Ashley tapped the button that activated it. Automatically it expanded upward until it was just under the level of the roof. Gripping the closest rung, Ashley turned to Jake. "I'll go up first, then you. Nog next, and T'Ara last." To Jake, she added: "Turn on the light now, but keep it at a low setting, okay?"

"I guess," he agreed. "You're in charge."

"I know." She grinned. "Okay, be very quiet." She climbed up the ladder and stopped just below the ceiling. Reaching up, she pushed at the tile. It moved up an inch or so, then she slid it to the side. There was a gap in the ceiling of about a foot and a half square. She looked down, pressing her finger to her lips, then clambered silently into the space. Jake followed her up the ladder. Poking his head into the gap, he saw Ashley waiting for him. She wiggled her fingers, and he handed over the flashlight. Then Nog tapped his ankles impatiently, so he climbed up beside Ashley.

There was a second ceiling about five feet above the first. Pipes and tubing ran all through the dark space here. There was light from the opening, and the light that Ashley held, but no more. Jake couldn't stand upright, and he felt uncomfortable crouched over. The piping that ran across the metal ceiling wasn't smooth, so he had to duck down to avoid hitting his head.

Nog slipped through the gap to join them, and a moment later Jake saw T'Ara arrive. Ashley nodded, and then gestured ahead with the dull beam of the flashlight she held. Then she started out, the rest of them falling in close behind her.

It was a weird walk. The pipes and tubes were all around, glimmering slightly in the faint light Ashley held. The floor beneath Jake's feet was metal but dull and unpolished. This was obviously some sort of old access passage to the inner workings of the station. Since it was cramped and unlit, it couldn't be one anyone used much.

They had walked twenty or thirty feet in silence when Ashley held up a hand and shone the light on it, so that they could all see she was stopping. Jake stood still and peered over her shoulder. Nog and T'Ara crowded in behind them.

They had reached a short side passage. Ashley nodded toward it, and Jake saw that there was a bundle on the floor here, nestled between the piping. Set on top of tubes and pipes were several dishes and spoons, a computer pad, and several other small items. There were pieces of what looked like girl's clothing, in a very long, thin style. Jake realized suddenly that they had to be the items Garak had reported stolen.

Ashley shone the beam of her flashlight on the bundle on the floor. Jake saw that it wasn't simply discarded clothing—it was a sleeping pad, and curled up on it was a dark figure. As the light flickered across the sleeping person, the eyes opened, and one arm went up to cover them.

"It's okay," Ashley said quickly. "We're not gonna hurt you."

Jake whistled with surprise as the figure in the bed suddenly jumped up and seemed to unwind. It was a girl—tall, slender, with long dark hair that hung down her back. But the most obvious thing of all was the gray reptilian skin. "She's a Cardassian," he said, amazed.

Ashley gave him a grin. "I told you it wasn't anyone we knew." To the Cardassian she said: "Can you understand us?"

The girl lowered her hand as her eyes adjusted to the light. "Yes," she said. Jake could hear the fear in her voice. "What do you want? What are you going to do to me?" She was trying to be brave, but he realized she was hardly any older than Ashley.

"We won't hurt you," Jake told her. "I promise."

"We just want to talk," Ashley explained. She shook her head in amazement. "How long have you been here?"

The Cardassian girl shrugged, and then scratched sleepily at her neck. "Nine days."

"You hid out when that Cardassian freighter was here!" Nog exclaimed.

The girl nodded. "Yes."

"But why?" asked T'Ara, puzzled.

Before the girl could reply, Jake broke in. "Look, I don't know about you lot, but I'm getting a crick in my neck standing here like this. Can we either sit down or go down into the classroom?"

The Cardassian girl was even taller than he was, and she was almost bent double. "It's okay with me," she agreed. She grabbed the tunic next to her bed and slipped it on over the T-shirt she wore. "It would be nice to straighten up."

"Back we go," said Nog with a sigh. "I hate all this walking."

"Stop grumbling," T'Ara told him. "It's good for you." She led the way this time, back down the passageway to the ladder. She scuttled down it quickly, and the others followed her.

In the well-lit classroom Jake could see the Cardassian girl properly for the first time. Like that of the others of her race, her skin was grayish, and there was a bony ridge on her forehead. Her eyes were a pale yellow color. There was another bony ridge down either side of her long neck. Her hands were long and her fingers thin. She was clenching and unclenching them nervously. It was obvious that though she was trying to act brave, she was quite scared.

"My name's Jake," he told her. "This is Ashley and T'Ara. That's Nog. What's your name?"

"Kam," she replied. "Kam Gavron. I guess you're wondering what I'm doing here, right?"

"Actually," Ashley admitted, "there's one question I've *got* to know the answer to. Why did you keep reprogramming the food replicator to make stew and cheesecake?"

Kam looked down at the floor. "Well, it's not what I *really* wanted," she said. "I was trying to get it to make my favorite food—we call it *k'aatch*—but the replicators won't make Cardassian food anymore."

Ashley nodded. "I know. My mom helped Chief O'Brien to reprogram them all. Nobody here likes Cardassian food. It's kind of disgusting sometimes."

"Well," Kam continued, "stew and cheesecake is sort of like *k'aatch,* if you don't look at it. It's the only thing I could eat here. I've been living on it."

"For nine days?" asked Nog, astonished. "You must be sick of it. I'm sick just *looking* at it."

"It is getting kind of monotonous," admitted Kam. "But it's that or nothing."

"I think I'd prefer to starve," muttered Nog.

"Okay," said Jake, "now we've got that sorted out, maybe you'll tell us just what you're doing here, Kam. Why did you stay behind, and what were you doing in the ceiling?"

"It's kind of complicated," Kam answered. "But if you were Cardassian—or even Bajoran—you'd have recognized my name."

"We would?" asked T'Ara, puzzled. "Why?"

Kam sighed. "My father is Gul Gavron." She looked at them and frowned. "Don't you know who he is?"

"Not really," admitted Ashley. "We don't know that much about your people."

"I guess not." Kam shook her head. "I'm so used to *everyone* knowing who he is. He's the hero of Mintos Alpha—Gul of the Third Fleet."

"Gul?" echoed Jake. "You mean he's one of the top people in the Cardassian space fleet?"

"Yes," Kam said with a little pride in her voice. "And if he ever finds out what I've done, he'll probably kill me."

CHAPTER 8

Jake stared at the skinny Cardassian girl. "Tell us all about it," he suggested.

Nodding, Kam sat down at one of the desks. The others took up seats about her. After biting her lower lip for a few seconds while she got her thoughts in order, Kam finally started. "You probably don't know what it's like on Cardassia," she said. Jake could hear the pain in her voice. "The military run our world, and almost all of the people have to work for them. Cardassia isn't a very rich world, so we rely on our colony planets for almost everything, including food. If the military is winning their battles, we have plenty of everything. If they aren't, we have shortages of all kinds—especially food." She sighed. "There have been lots of days when I've had next to nothing to eat. After that, even stew and cheesecake every day tastes great."

"It must be horrible there," Ashley said. "Why do you stand it? Why doesn't anyone stop the military?"

"Are you kidding?" asked Kam. "They have all the

weapons, all the ships—everything. If you even say a word against them, you can get beaten up or even killed. Even if you're one of the family members of the leaders. We have to do what we're told. And the military controls the schools, too. Every lesson we get is approved by the War Council. We're told that the Federation is a war-loving group of planets out to kill all Cardassians and steal our worlds."

"That's not true!" T'Ara said, forgetting she wasn't supposed to get angry. "The Federation wants peace and every race to help each other."

"Yes, but *Cardassians* aren't told that," Kam explained. "If they were, then maybe they wouldn't want to keep the army in power. So we're all told what monsters everybody here is, and how you kill and torture Cardassians for fun. Most people believe it and are terrified of you. They think that the space navy is the only thing that is saving them from being killed. That's another reason why everyone puts up with the military.

"Well, like I said, my father is one of the highest people in the space navy. He's Gul of the Third Fleet and really important. So we did get a bit better treatment at home than most people would. And we were always told what a hero he was and everything. But I wasn't always sure about that, because he had a real bad temper sometimes. If anybody annoyed him, he'd just hit them and keep on hitting them until he was too tired to do it anymore. He used to hit my mother and my older brother. Sometimes he hit me, too, but mostly he wasn't so bad with me. I don't really know why, but he seemed to think I was more like him than my brother was.

"He was always telling me how wonderful all the battles he fought were, and how we were beating the Federation and everything. But he never really sounded like he meant it, you know? Like he was trying to believe it but knew better. I couldn't help thinking that if he was wrong about hitting us all, then maybe he was wrong about fighting the Federation. I always wondered if everybody here was as bad as he claimed.

"Anyway, on my last birthday, he brought me to the spacedocks and showed me some of the ships there. He was very proud of them and how fast they were. He told me how many other ships each of them had blown up and how powerful they were. I think he thought I'd be really impressed, but it just made me very sad that all they were meant to do was to kill other people.

"There were a couple of dirty-looking ships there. When I asked him about them, he told me that they were freighters, mostly for the various colony worlds. Then he got called away because of some sort of problem, and he left me with one of his young officers, called Tak." She gave a sad smile. "He's a nice kind of person, and I always got along well with him. I hope he didn't get in trouble because of me."

Jake was startled: Kam sounded for once just like Riv, who hadn't wanted to get anyone else in trouble because of what *he'd* done. Weird!

"Well," Kam continued, "Tak showed me one of the freighters they were loading up. He let me watch them and told me it was going to be coming here to Deep Space Nine. That was really interesting for me. Back on

Cardassia, everyone was told that the Bajorans were a bunch of cowards and traitors who had worked with the Federation to sell us out. And we were told that Deep Space Nine was stolen from us. But I never really believed those stories, because I'd heard my father talking with other soldiers. I overheard them say that they'd actually handed over Deep Space Nine themselves because they thought it was useless. And that the Bajorans had been innocent, and that *we* had invaded them.

"That made me kind of ashamed, because I'd always hated the Federation as a kid. I'd been terribly angry that you were all trying to invade and kill us. Then I heard my father saying that *we* had done that to Bajor. I began to wonder how many other lies I'd been told. The more I looked at the freighter, the more I wanted to be on it. I wanted to come here and see for myself what things were *really* like. I wanted to know if the people in the Federation were *really* monsters. I wanted to know the *truth,* just for once." Kam sounded very angry.

"So," asked Ashley, "how did you get aboard?"

"Well," Kam continued, "my father returned, and he was really mad about something. He called Tak to one side. Poor Tak had to stand there and get yelled at—and I'll bet it was for something he hadn't even done. I wasn't being watched, so I screwed up all of my courage and I slipped away. I managed to get to one of the containers of supplies that were being loaded." She gave a slight smile. "I'm kind of good at working computers. That's how I could figure out how to fix the replicators. I snuck inside the container and then waited.

"I was horribly afraid that my father or Tak would realize I'd gone and figure out where I was. But somehow they didn't. Instead, a little while later, the container was loaded on the freighter. Some time after that the ship took off. I waited till the ship was under way, and then I slipped out of the container and hid inside the ship. The freighter took about a day to get here. When it arrived, I got back into the container and just waited to be unloaded. I've been hiding ever since."

After a moment's silence Nog shook his head. "Wow! You must be really brave to do something like that!"

"Not really," Kam told him, smiling a little. "I was terribly scared most of the time."

"But you came here," T'Ara said. "Where you'd always been told we were monsters and terrible people. That *was* very brave, even if you didn't really believe we were all that dreadful."

"But why did you hide inside the schoolroom ceiling?" asked Jake.

Kam looked a little sad. "Well, I didn't dare let myself be seen at first. But I know how these kinds of space stations are made. My father had to oversee some of them being built, so I'd found some plans. I knew there were lots of places I could hide, but I also wanted to be able to find out what everybody here was really like. The first day or so I hid out near the docking ring. Then I spotted you and Nog, and I realized that there were people on the station who were my age. So I followed you back. I thought that the best way I could find out what you were like was to listen in on your classes. And I took one of the computers to study at night."

Ashley frowned at her. "And you took some clothing from Garak's shop, didn't you?"

Kam nodded. "I had to. You know how gross it is wearing the same thing every day for over a week? I was afraid you'd start to *smell* me down here."

Jake had to laugh at the thought. "You're really wild," he said. "So—*now* what do you think about the Federation?"

"Do you still think we're monsters?" asked T'Ara.

Kam shook her head firmly. "No, I don't. You all seemed to be nice people to me. And now that I've had a chance to talk to you, I *know* you're nice." She looked at them with hope. "I'd like to be friends—if you would."

"You bet," agreed Jake readily.

"Definitely," Ashley added.

"Okay by me," Nog said with a grin.

"It would be acceptable," finished T'Ara. Ashley darted a glare at the young girl, and T'Ara added: "I would like that, Kam."

The Cardassian girl gave a wide smile, then stood up and hugged each of them in turn. "Thank you," she said, wiping at the corners of her eyes. "I really am glad that we can be friends instead of enemies."

"But it does land us in trouble," Jake said. Four pairs of eyes stared at him. "Well, we can't just put you back in the ceiling and go on like nothing's happened," he explained. "My dad is in charge of this station, and he gave me and Nog a real talking-to last night."

Ashley nodded glumly. "And Ms. O'Brien knows we were trying to catch whoever was fixing the replicator," she put in. "We have to tell her *something,* or we'll be in for trouble."

"Also," T'Ara pointed out, "there is that clothing you stole from Garak. Sooner or later you will need more fresh clothing. You are not likely to get away with stealing it."

Nog chuckled. "I know what we could do," he suggested. "We could just blame the whole thing on Riv."

"But that is not true," T'Ara said.

Shrugging, Nog said, "Yeah—but if anyone deserves getting into trouble for something they didn't do, it's Riv."

Kam shook her head. "It's not right to blame anyone for what I've done."

"Maybe not," agreed Nog. "But it would be fun."

"No." Kam sighed. "I guess you're going to have to turn me in, then." She seemed very unhappy. "Do you think they'll make me go back to Cardassia? I *hate* it there! And I don't want to go back to my father!"

Ashley frowned and asked Jake, "Do you think your father might give her asylum? Then she could stay here."

Jake considered it. The Federation usually granted people's requests to stay if they were asked—but that was for adults. "I don't know if he can do that," he admitted. "After all, Kam is kind of young. Dad may not have any choice."

"But you could ask," said Ashley.

"Of course I can ask!" exclaimed Jake. "And I'm gonna—right now!" He turned to Kam. "I want you to be able to stay. And my dad is usually pretty reasonable about things. If anyone can think of something, he can."

Kam smiled a bit sadly. "It must be nice to have a father like that."

"It is," agreed Jake. "For the most part. When I do something dumb, though, I get it."

The Cardassian girl nodded. "But does he hit you, like mine does?"

"Never!" Jake realized how lucky he was to have such a parent. "Look, Nog and I will go and talk to my dad. I *know* he'll be sympathetic." He turned to Ashley. "Why don't you and T'Ara go and find Ms. O'Brien? She'll help."

"Right," agreed Ashley. "She's neat," she explained to Kam. "She'll help us."

"Okay," Jake finished. "Kam, when we're gone, you just hide again. School won't start for a little while yet, but it might be best if nobody knows you're here till we tell them."

Kam nodded. "All right." She looked at the four of them. "Thank you," she said simply. "I really appreciate what you're doing. No matter what happens, I'll never forget." There were definitely tears in her eyes now.

"Ah," growled Nog, "this is getting too soppy. That's what you get for making friends with girls."

Jake grinned as he headed for the door. "Let's get moving," he said. Nog scuttled along beside him. Ashley and T'Ara went with them as far as the first junction, then split off to go after the teacher.

None of them thought to look behind them. If they had, they might have seen Riv. He slipped inside the classroom. He'd been listening outside the door for a while, and now there was a big smile on his face.

CHAPTER 9

Jake had not been in Ops very many times. This was the control center of Deep Space Nine, where his father had his office and from where the entire station was run. Jake and Nog looked nervously about the room in front of them as they stepped off the turbolift.

The main floor was circular, with a huge control panel in the center. Above this, dominating the room, was the main scanner. It wasn't working at the moment, so it looked like a large archway spanning almost to the ceiling. Around the main floor was a wide catwalk with further workstations on it. Opposite the lift was the doorway that led to the commander's office.

There was plenty of low-level talking and a lot of computer and other mechanical noises in the room. There were about twenty people at workstations, all looking very busy. Jake recognized Ms. O'Brien's husband, Chief O'Brien, over at one control panel. His father's friend, Dax, was bent over her science board. She looked pretty human—except for a band of thick freckles that started at her temples and ran down the sides of her face and neck—but she was actually a Trill, a joined species. Inside her was a small creature that shared her mind and body, so Dax was both very old and yet also a pretty young woman.

In the center of the room was Major Kira. She wore the Bajoran uniform and stood with her hands clasped behind her back, staring over her panels. Her brown hair was short, and she wore a Bajoran earring in her right ear. She was a Bajoran soldier who had fought the Cardassians, and she sometimes seemed to forget that she didn't have to fight everybody she met. Facing her across the main control panel was Jake's father.

"Jake," he called out. "What brings you up here? Isn't it time you were at school?"

Several of the other people in the room looked up at them. Jake caught sight of a quick smile from Dax. "Uh, yeah, but . . ." He took a deep breath and plunged on. "You told me to come to you any time if I had a problem."

His father glanced down at the control panel. "This isn't a good time, Jake," he said. "We're having trouble with the sensors. How urgent is it?"

Jake said, "Kind of important."

Commander Sisko considered this for a moment, then nodded. "Carry on with the check, please, Major," he said.

Kira nodded. "Aye, sir." She turned back to her panel, ignoring the two youngsters.

Commander Sisko crossed the room to join Jake and

Nog. Everyone else went back to his or her duties. "Well?" he said, looking from one to the other.

Jake wanted his father on Kam's side. "Can we offer sanctuary to a Cardassian?" he asked.

His father looked puzzled. "If I'm asked, and if the person hasn't committed any crimes, then we're always willing to offer asylum. Is this just an academic question, or is there a reason behind it?"

"Well," Jake admitted, "there is a reason. We've found a Cardassian hiding on the station. She wants to stay here, but she's afraid you'll insist she has to go back to Cardassia."

"And why would she think that?" his father asked. *"Is* she a criminal? And how did you happen just to find her?"

Jake shifted uncomfortably. "She's not exactly a *criminal,"* he said. "And Ashley Fontana and T'Ara found her. She'd been messing with the replicator."

His father sighed. "Not *exactly* a criminal?" he repeated. "Well, what exactly is she?"

"She's the one who stole the stuff from Garak's shop," Jake told him. "But she didn't have any choice."

"Ah." Understanding was dawning on his father now. "This noncriminal of yours is a young girl, I take it, since it was young girl's clothing that was stolen?" Jake nodded. "I'm starting to see the problem. Just how young is she?"

"About my age," Jake admitted.

His father rubbed his chin. "Jake," he said gently, "that *could* be a problem. She is still a child, and we can't simply let runaway children stay here on the station. She really ought to be back with her parents."

"She *hates* her father," Nog offered helpfully. "She doesn't want to go back."

Jake nodded. "And I told her you'd do your best to help," he added. "I know you will, Dad."

His father smiled. "Jake, I appreciate your faith in me. And I promise to try and live up to it. Now—"

"Commander!" It was Major Kira calling out loudly from the main control panel. "We've got some of the sensors back. And we've got trouble. *Big* trouble."

Dax whirled about in her chair. "I confirm, Commander. I'm reading eight Galor-class battleships approaching the station."

"Eight?" Commander Sisko scowled. "Why are eight Cardassian warships here? Dax, open a channel to the lead ship."

The big holoscreen in the center of the room lit up. Jake gasped as he stared directly into the face of a Cardassian soldier. The warrior was seated in a large thronelike chair on the main deck of his battleship. He was thin, gray, and looked very angry indeed.

"This is Commander Sisko, in charge of Deep Space Nine," his father called out. "Is there something we can do for you"—his eyes flickered over the badges on the armor the soldier wore—"Gul?"

"Yes," hissed the Gul. "There is indeed something you can do for me, Sisko. You can return my daughter to me."

Jake felt his stomach ache. His father glanced down at

him, and then back at the scowling Cardassian soldier on the screen.

"I'm not certain I quite understand you," he said. "What is your daughter doing here?"

"She's been kidnapped," the Cardassian growled. "I want her back safely, and I want the criminals responsible handed over to be punished."

"I see." Jake's father nodded. "I will investigate and get back to you."

"You will do more than investigate," the Cardassian

77

snarled. "You will act. I warn you, Sisko, that if my daughter is not returned safely to me within one of your hours, I will destroy your station!" The picture went dead.

After a moment's silence Chief O'Brien muttered, "Well, they don't mince words, do they?"

Dax looked across at the commander. "The Cardassian ships are powering up their weapon systems, Commander," she reported in a calm voice. "Their phasers are coming on line."

Chief O'Brien muttered something under his breath. Then, louder, he asked, "Shall I raise our shields, sir?"

Jake's father shook his head. "No, Chief. Not yet. We don't want to look like we're asking for trouble. If his daughter really is on board the station, he won't risk firing until we respond to him. I think we're safe for now." He stared down at his son and Nog as Major Kira moved to join them. "I assume you know what this means?"

"We're in trouble?" asked Nog. He glared at Jake. "How come we're *always* in trouble?"

"No," the Commander said quickly, "that's not what I meant." He looked at Jake. "Is this Cardassian you've found his daughter?"

"Uh, I guess she might be," Jake said. "If he's Gul Gavron."

"Gavron . . ." Major Kira said, her voice almost a squeak. "If that's Gul Gavron . . ."

"We're in really deep trouble," agreed Jake's father.

He sighed. "I think you'd better tell us everything, Jake, from the beginning."

"Okay." Jake did so, in as much detail as he could remember. When he'd told the story, he finished up: "But he's lying, Dad. Kam wasn't kidnapped—she ran away."

"So it would seem," his father agreed. "What do you think, Major?"

The Bajoran officer scowled. "I think he's too proud to admit that his daughter was unhappy enough to run away. Saying she was kidnapped shifts the blame onto other people."

"You could be right." The commander thought about it. "But it leaves us with a very nasty problem, doesn't it?"

Kira nodded. "He wants us to produce nonexistent kidnappers for him to punish. We *can't* do that!"

"No, we can't," Jake's father agreed. "And if we don't, he might well attack the station to cover up his shame. Cardassians can be very touchy about things like that."

"Tell me about it," Kira replied. "I've fought them. So what *are* we going to do?"

"*You* are in charge here for now," Commander Sisko told her. "If Gul Gavron calls with any more demands, stall him." He glanced down at Jake and Nog. "You two had better take me to this young friend of yours. It looks as if she may have gotten us all into a whole heap of trouble."

* * *

They were getting close to the schoolroom when Jake suddenly saw Ashley, T'Ara, and Ms. O'Brien heading toward them through the crowd of people in the Promenade. As soon as she saw Jake, Ashley waved.

"Jake!" she called. Her voice sounded really worried. "It's Kam—she's disappeared!"

CHAPTER 10

Jake's father frowned. "Disappeared?" he repeated. "You mean she's hiding again?"

T'Ara shook her head. "We do not know."

"We left her in the classroom," Ashley added. "And when we got back with Ms. O'Brien, there was no sign of her."

"Did you check in the ceiling?" asked Jake.

Ashley glared at him. "Of course we did," she replied. "Do you think we're *stupid?*"

"This," said Commander Sisko, "is not good. Not good at all."

Ms. O'Brien looked puzzled. "Surely one young Cardassian girl at loose somewhere on the station isn't a problem?" she asked.

"Normally," Jake's father said, "I'd agree with you. But there are eight Cardassian warships surrounding us, and her father is in command. He wants Kam back or he'll destroy us."

T'Ara gasped. Then, catching herself, she said, "That is not logical. She would be destroyed, too."

"You're quite right," the commander told her. "But I don't think Gul Gavron is interested in logic. Kam has caused him pain, and he wants to hurt someone. Preferably us."

"Then we have to find her," said Ms. O'Brien. She looked at her students. "Do you have any idea where she might have gone?"

Jake tried to imagine, but he came up blank. "I don't think she *would* wander off," he said. "She agreed to wait for us."

"Maybe," suggested Nog, "she just disliked the idea of going home so much that she changed her mind."

"That does not make sense," T'Ara objected. "She must realize that now we know of her existence, we could use the sensors to find her."

"A good idea," agreed Commander Sisko. He tapped the communicator on his chest. "Sisko to Dax."

From the air came a disembodied reply. "Dax here."

"Can you use the sensors to sweep the station?" Jake's father asked. "We seem to have temporarily misplaced the Cardassian girl."

There was a slight pause, and then Dax's reply floated out of the air: "I'm sorry, Commander. We're still having trouble with the sensors. If we have a biological scan of her, we might be able to do it, but without one I don't think there's a chance."

"Terrific." Commander Sisko scowled, deep in thought. "Stand by. Sisko out." He shook his head. "I suppose we could try and get a trace of her from her hiding place," he suggested to Ms. O'Brien.

"There's no need for that, sir," said Ashley quickly. "I already have a bioscan for Kam. I got one when I set a trap on the replicator."

"Well done," said the commander warmly. "Where is it?"

Ashley was blushing at the praise. "In my computer pad. I left it in the classroom."

"Okay," the commander said. "Go fetch it and bring it up to Ops. We can plug it in there and scan the entire station."

Ashley nodded and spun round. She started off for the classroom. Jake, Nog, and T'Ara went with her. As they ran through the crowded Promenade, Jake realized that very few people knew about the threatened attack yet. It was probably best. The last thing they needed right now was panic. But if they couldn't find Kam, then everyone would have to be told. . . .

They reached the classroom just as the other students began to arrive for class. "There it is," Ashley said, pointing to the computer pad she'd left on her desk. As she hurried over to collect it, Nog gave a cry of pleasure. He scuttled forward and scooped something up off the floor. Jake just caught a glimpse of something shiny before Nog's hand closed over it.

"What's that?" he asked curiously.

"Mine!" said Nog. "I found it."

"I'm not claiming it," Jake replied. The Ferengi believed in the old saying about "Finders keepers" with all their greedy little hearts. "I just want to know what it is."

Nog clutched his find to his chest, suspicious. Then he nodded. "Okay," he agreed. He opened his fingers just a few inches. "It's an earring."

There was something about it that struck a chord in Jake's memory. "I've seen it somewhere before," he said slowly.

Nog clenched his fist over it again. "Hey, I told you—it's mine. I don't care what stories you make up to pretend you lost it."

"Not *me*," said Jake with a sigh. "But I know I've seen that earring before."

"Who cares?" asked Ashley. "I've got the pad, so let's go."

"It might be important," said Jake. "I'm sure it wasn't here earlier, was it?"

"No way," said Nog. "I'd have seen it if it had been."

"That's for sure," agreed Ashley. "You can spot a speck of gold at fifty miles."

Nog grinned at the thought. "Yeah. I'm real good at finding treasure."

"That's not treasure," Jake said, finally remembering where he'd seen it before. "That's Riv's earring."

"No, it isn't," insisted Nog. "It's *mine*. I found it."

"No, you don't understand," Jake said urgently. "It's the earring that Riv got from his father."

"So?" Ashley was impatient to go. "He must have dropped it, that's all. Come on!"

"In a minute," Jake insisted. "That earring was Riv's

most valuable possession—his only memory of his parents, he said. He wouldn't just lose it and not search for it. Unless . . ."

T'Ara grinned, then switched to raising her eyebrow instead. "Unless something else distracted him," she finished. "Like Kam."

"Right!" Jake was certain it made sense. "He must have come in here and found her. And we all know how he hates Cardassians. . . ."

Ashley went pale. "You think he attacked her?"

"Yeah." Jake didn't like to think of the implications. "And in the struggle his earring fell off. He didn't notice it right away."

"Come on," snapped Ashley. "If he's kidnapped her, then we've *really* got to get this sample to your father. Who knows what he'll do to her?"

Jake nodded. "And we know exactly what her father will do to this station if he doesn't get her back. . . ."

They ran all the way back to the turbolift. There were a few annoyed yells as they pushed through the crowd in the Promenade, but for once Jake was certain he wouldn't be in trouble over that. The four of them piled into the lift, and Jake yelled, "Ops!" It seemed to crawl up the shaft, and he found himself tapping his foot impatiently on the floor. Then it arrived, and they spilled out into the control room.

"I've got the sample," Ashley announced, holding up her pad.

"Good." Dax stood up and beckoned to her. "Over here, please."

They all went over. Dax gave them one of her dazzling smiles, gently taking the pad from Ashley. She took a link line from her control panel and tapped it into the pad. The computer screen on her panel shifted to give new patterns and readings. Dax's fingers flew over the controls as she set the main computer to getting the information out of Ashley's pad.

"Got it," she murmured. She tapped in further commands. Jake, Nog, T'Ara, and Ashley leaned over the screens. On the main viewscreen in the center of the room, the Cardassian flagship was visible—a grim reminder of what awaited them if Dax couldn't trace Kam. On the small panel they saw a cross section of Deep Space Nine displayed. The computer narrowed down the picture, and then zoomed in to a single spot.

"There she is," said Dax. "I've got a clear reading."

"Where is she?" Commander Sisko called. He was at the main console, next to Major Kira.

"In the Promenade," Dax replied. Then she frowned. "No . . . she's not *in* it. She's *above* it. She seems to be located just inside the ceiling ducts."

"Apparently she's very fond of ceilings," the commander said.

Jake shook his head. "I don't think she's likely to be too fond of this one," he told his father. "I think Riv's got her."

His father frowned. "Riv? What would he want with her?"

The terrible feeling that Jake had been experiencing

finally found words. "He hates Cardassians. I think he's taken her up there to kill her."

Major Kira looked very worried. "And if he *does* kill her," she said, "then he's killing us as well." She gestured at the main screen. "Those ships are sure to attack us then."

CHAPTER 11

Kam swallowed and tried not to look down from her wobbly perch. She tried to fight the giddiness that threatened to make her lose her grip and send her falling to her death below.

Riv grinned at her. The height didn't seem to bother him. "Scared, huh?" he sneered. "Just like all Cardassians."

She refused to be baited. While she was waiting for Jake and his friends, this strange Bajoran boy had attacked her and dragged her along with him. She'd tried to fight, but he was much stronger than she was, and it hadn't done her much good. Riv now had a couple of blood-red gashes across his face where she'd managed to scratch him. She had a dull pain in her side where he'd punched her to force her to stop fighting.

"Why are you doing this to me?" she asked.

This seemed to amuse him. "Whining, eh? Go ahead, beg for your life. You never know, it might get you somewhere." He shrugged. "Then again, I might push

you off anyway." He made a sudden motion with his hand. Kam squealed and shied away from him, gripping the thin rail beneath her for support. Riv laughed—a nasty, harsh sound.

She took a deep breath and stared back at him. "I *won't* beg," she told him. "If you're going to kill me, you'll kill me anyway. I just want to know *why* you're doing it. I've done nothing to you."

His face twisted into a dark scowl. "Your people have!" he told her angrily. "They killed both of my parents! I spent all my life in hiding, fighting Cardassians."

Kam was ashamed for her people. "I'm really sorry about your parents. But why pick on *me?*"

"Sorry? You?" Riv shook his head. "I don't believe it. You Cardassians don't have any *honest* emotions. You're just trash. And I'm going to make you all pay—starting with you."

Kam swallowed again. The urge to look down was almost irresistible, but she knew that if she did she'd lose her balance and fall. "So you're going to kill me for revenge?" She shrugged. "Well, I can't say I blame you. If I'd loved my parents the way you must have, I'd probably hate the people who did it."

"Oh, no," he said. "You can't get me thinking you care. It's just a trick. Anyway, I'm not gonna kill you unless I have to. I heard you tell those other kids that you're the daughter of a Gul. You're worth a lot to me alive."

Kam managed a weak smile back. "Yes? Then this

isn't the best place to keep me. I could fall off any second."

"If you do, you do." He didn't sound bothered. "I've been trying to contact the Bajoran underground to join it. I want to fight against the Cardassians, just like my parents did. But so far I haven't been able to get through to them."

Puzzled, Kam said, "The war's over. Bajor's free. Surely there isn't any underground now?"

Riv gave a harsh laugh. "That's what everyone tries to tell me, but it isn't true. We may have got our planet back, but *true* Bajorans won't rest till we've wiped every last Cardassian from the face of the universe. There *has* to be an underground. And if I can offer you to them— the daughter of a Gul as a hostage—then they're bound to let me join, aren't they?"

"The war is over," she told him. "We're at peace."

"Peace?" He sounded very bitter. "I'll never be at peace while there's one Cardassian still alive. We're still at war, whatever the Federation or anyone else might say."

"You're still at war," Kam said, realizing this was Riv's problem. He'd lived filled with hatred and fear and fighting for so long that he didn't know any other way. He wouldn't accept that things had changed. "Riv, we don't have to be enemies. We can be friends."

He laughed. "The only way to make peace with your enemies is to kill them."

"Maybe that's what your parents told you," Kam said gently, "but it's not true. There's another way. You stop being enemies and start being friends."

"Friends?" Riv looked as if he wanted to spit at her. "Cardassians don't have any friends. You're *animals,* that's all."

"What if everybody is right," Kam asked him, "and there isn't an underground carrying on the war against the Cardassians? What if there really *is* peace?"

"Then you'd better get ready to die," he told her. "Because you're either coming down from here with me to go to the underground, or I'm going to make at least one Cardassian pay for what they've done to my people and to me."

There was the sound of someone clearing his throat. It came from behind Riv. He looked around, and Kam could just see past him. The beam that they were perched on went into the far wall as it curved up to touch the roof. Riv had removed a panel in that wall and forced her through it and out onto the beam. When he'd followed her, he'd left the panel open. Over his shoulder she could see that there were several people standing there, in the small access corridor. One of them was staring down at them through the hole. He was tall and dark-skinned, dressed in a Starfleet uniform. She guessed that he had to be Jake's father. Behind him were Jake, Nog, and Odo.

"Hello, Riv," the commander said quietly. "Hello, Kam. Don't be alarmed."

Riv shook his head. "I'm not alarmed," he said. "You should be, though. I want to talk to Major Kira."

"I'm afraid that's not possible," Commander Sisko replied. "Major Kira is in Ops. We have a bit of a problem on our hands right now."

"Yeah," Riv agreed. "Me."

The commander sighed. "You are part of it, yes. Now, please—I don't know why you're out there, but come back in. Let Kam come back in."

"No," said Riv firmly. "You've got two choices. Bring Major Kira here, or I push this Cardassian off the beam. Make up your mind—now!" He lunged out, and his hand closed over Kam's shoulder. She fought to stop herself screaming and to stay on the thin beam.

Jake gasped as he saw Riv get ready to push Kam from the beam. They were so high up out there that she would certainly be killed if she fell. "Don't do it, Riv!" he yelled. He looked at his father. "Maybe I can talk sense to him," he suggested.

His father thought for a moment, then nodded. "Though I doubt anyone can talk sense to that boy," he muttered.

Slipping past his father in the narrow confines of the access tunnel, Jake peered out of the hole. The beam looked even thinner from here, and he could see it was bending visibly under the weight of Riv and Kam. It was meant to carry decorations and banners for festivals, not to support people.

Behind him he heard his father ask Odo in a quiet voice that Riv wouldn't be able to hear, "Could you change shape and go out there, Odo? As a mouse or something?"

"I'm afraid not," Odo replied. "I may be able to take on the *shape* and *size* of a mouse, but I'd still have the *weight* of a man. Riv's picked his place very carefully. If

93

I go out there, the beam will probably break. One of the youngsters might be able to go out, but no adult."

"I don't think he'd sit and watch anyone crawl out there," Jake's father said with a sigh.

Nog cleared his throat. "What about using the transporter to beam them in here?" he suggested brightly.

"A good idea," Commander Sisko replied. Nog beamed, but his face fell when the commander added, "If we weren't having sensor problems. We're going to have to rely on talking him into giving up."

That was Jake's cue, he knew. "Hi, Riv," he said, hoping for some inspiration. "Aren't you going a bit far this time?"

"Nice joke, jerk," Riv answered. "I *am* out pretty far, aren't I?"

Jake could see the fear on Kam's face and in her eyes. He guessed from the tense way she gripped the beam that she was probably afraid of heights. "Why don't you let her go?" he asked.

"No way," Riv said. "She's my ticket out of here."

"I thought you were supposed to be brave," Jake sneered.

"I'm braver than you!" Riv yelled back, annoyed and red in the face.

"Yeah?" asked Jake. "Then why are you putting her through this?"

"She's a Cardassian!" yelled Riv.

"And you're just a coward!" Jake howled back.

For a moment Jake thought he'd annoyed Riv enough for the Bajoran to come inside just to beat his brains out. Riv's fists clenched and unclenched. But then he shook his head. "It won't work," he said. "I'll kill her if I have to. I promise you."

"Then you'll kill us all," Jake told him.

Riv stared at him suspiciously, obviously expecting a trick. "What are you talking about?"

"You know she's Gul Gavron's daughter?" asked Jake.

"Yeah." Riv grinned again. "A pretty neat hostage."

"Well, he's *here* and he wants her back."

"What?" Both Kam and Riv said this at the same time. It was hard for Jake to decide who looked more surprised.

"He's in space just off the station," Jake explained. "With eight warships. He wants Kam back, and he says if he doesn't get her, he'll blow up Deep Space Nine."

Kam gasped, but Riv just gave a short barklike laugh. "He's not crazy enough to do that!"

"You don't know my father," Kam said with real anger and hatred in her voice. "If he's mad enough, he'll do anything."

Riv thought about that for a minute. "This station has Federation people on it," he said. "If the admiral blows it up, wouldn't the Federation declare war on Cardassia?"

"Probably," agreed Jake. "But that wouldn't exactly help us. We'd all be dead."

"It would help *me*," Riv said. There was a very odd look in his eye. "I'm not afraid to die. And if the Gul blows up Deep Space Nine, then the Federation would go to war with the Cardassians. The Federation's bound to win and wipe the stinking scum out." He laughed. "It sounds like a pretty good deal to me."

"What?" Kam looked furious now, not as scared as she had been. "Is that all you can think about? Killing Cardassians? Well, you can kill *me* if you like, but I'm not gonna let you kill the other people on the station. They're good people—Jake and Ashley and T'Ara and Nog and all the rest. They don't deserve to die, just so you can start a stupid war! I won't let you kill them!" With a growl she lunged at Riv.

Jake was terrified. Kam was mad enough to send both herself and Riv plunging to their deaths. "Stop it!" he yelled, scared of what might happen. "Kam, don't do it!"

She hesitated, on her feet now, balancing on the beam. She seemed to have forgotten about her fear of heights, she was so mad with Riv. The Bajoran boy was just as changed as she was. He stared at her, obviously puzzled and shocked. "You want to save their lives?" he said, his voice with an odd catch to it.

"They're my friends," she growled. "And I won't let you get them killed."

"But . . . you're a *Cardassian*," he said, struggling with the idea. "Cardassians hate *everybody*."

"Well, *I* don't!" she yelled. "Right now there are only two people I hate. One's my father, and the other is you."

Jake could see that Riv was finally starting to see how wrong he'd been. "Riv," he said gently. "It's true. She means it. She *is* our friend. I don't care if she's a Cardassian or whatever. She's a neat person. And she's a whole lot nicer than you are."

Riv turned on the beam. Jake could see that the Bajoran boy's face was twisted and twitching.

"Come on, Riv," Nog called over Jake's shoulder. "Come on inside. Let Kam come in." He winced, then added, "Please!"

As Riv stood there, struggling with himself, Kam gave a sharp laugh. "Yeah. If you really want to hurt me, let me go in. I'll have to go back to my father. He's probably going to kill me for running away."

Jake watched, hardly daring to breathe. He could feel his father, Nog, and Odo standing behind him, watching as well. Would Riv agree? Would he come in?

Ashley stared across the Ops room in awe. She'd always wanted to be up here, checking out some of the terrifically neat machinery. Now she wished she were somewhere else. On a nice, safe planet for example.

Major Kira was standing in front of the main viewer. Gul Gavron's huge figure was staring back from the projection at her. "We're doing our best," the major said, trying to smile. "It's just taking a little bit longer than we thought to find your daughter."

"Then your best is obviously not good enough!" Gul Gavron roared. He was hissing, and his face was twitching. Ashley could see he was definitely mad. "So I'll give you a little incentive." Turning to one of his officers offscreen, he yelled, "Fire a warning shot at the station!"

"At once, sir," a voice replied.

Major Kira whirled around. "Raise shields! Full! Battle stations! We're under attack!"

CHAPTER 12

Jake stared at Riv, who was still standing on the beam. The young Bajoran was clearly fighting a battle with his beliefs. Quietly Jake asked his father, "Do you think he's going to let her go?"

"I think so," his father whispered back. "He only has to accept the truth that his hatred was wrong. He's been fighting a war all his life, and he's been a prisoner of a peace he doesn't understand or accept. He's grown up hating all Cardassians. But he's discovered that at least one of them is a good person. It's hard to keep your hatred going when the person you're trying to hate has a face—and a good heart."

It made sense to Jake; he only hoped it was the same conclusion that Riv would reach.

Finally the Bajoran boy nodded. "Okay," he said. "We're coming in. She's not a bad person, is she?"

"Great!" Jake gave him a big smile. "You're not so bad yourself."

Riv started to turn. As he did so, the alarms began to

sound. Major Kira's voice came over the public address system. "Red alert! We're under attack!"

Something hit the station's force-shields. The energy field absorbed the blow, but for a second the power blinked, and the inertial dampers failed. The deck beneath Jake's feet shook as if it were an earthquake.

On the beam Riv gave a strangled cry of surprise and lost his footing.

Jake saw Riv stumble and then fall. For one heart-stopping second, he was convinced that the Bajoran boy would die.

Then Kam flung herself forward. Her left hand wrapped about Riv's wrist, and her other circled the beam. With a cry of pain she fell sprawled across the beam. She clung tightly with her right arm, and just as tightly to Riv with her other hand.

Riv swung below her, a hundred feet above the floor. There was pain on his face—and fear. He glanced down and then upward. Kam's face was twisted in agony, and Jake saw that she was losing her grip on the beam.

"Let go!" Riv yelled at her. "If you don't, you're gonna fall, too! Let me go!"

"No," Kam snarled. "I'm not going to let you die."

"You can't help it!" Riv shouted. "There's no point in us both going!"

"No!"

Jake had been frozen to the spot, unable to move. As he watched Riv swinging in Kam's tight grip, he saw that she was losing her hold on the beam. Her arm wasn't strong enough to hold her weight and Riv's. Jake didn't

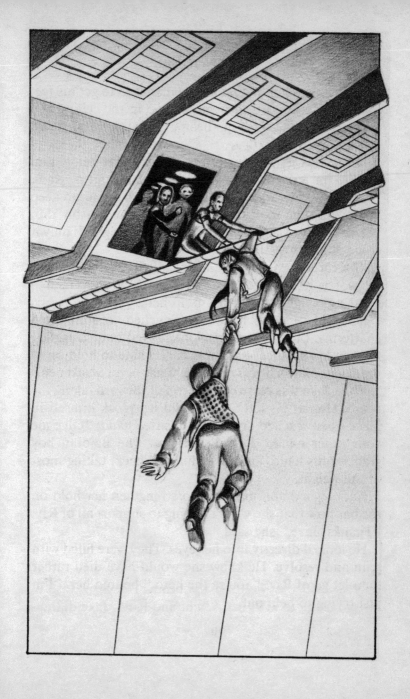

like heights much, but he finally managed to get his feet moving. He jumped through the gap in the ceiling and then stepped out onto the beam. Behind him, he heard Nog gasp.

One quick glimpse of the Promenade far below him made him jerk his head back up to look out at Kam. "Hang on!" he called. Slowly, his arms held out to keep his balance, he took small steps along the terribly thin beam. It sagged slightly under his added weight. If only it could stand this strain!

"Be careful, Jake," his father called. Jake could hear the worry in the voice. "Odo's getting some of his men to bring a portable tractor beam up here."

"Okay," he said, his teeth clenched to stop them chattering. Step by slow step, he moved out, struggling to keep his balance. Kam was barely able to hold on to the beam, but her grip on Riv's wrist never weakened.

Then Jake was close enough to fall forward, along the beam. He put his left arm around it to lock himself in place, then reached down with his free hand. "Give me your other hand," he ordered Riv. The Bajoran boy grabbed his hand, and Jake clutched back, taking most of the weight.

Kam sighed and managed to strengthen her hold on the bar now that she wasn't having to support all of Riv. "Thanks, Jake," she said.

He looked directly into her eyes. They were filled with pain and resolve. He knew she would have died rather than let go of Riv. "You're the hero," he told her. "I'm just trying to help out."

Then he felt a strange sensation, as if invisible fingers were enfolding him.

"Got them," said Odo's voice with deep satisfaction. The portable tractor beam must have arrived. "All right," the constable called. "You can let go of the beam now. We've got all three of you locked in."

It was one of the hardest things Jake had ever done to loosen his hold on the beam. He was terribly afraid that when he did, he would fall and then smash into the floor far, far below. But he knew he could trust Odo. He let go.

And didn't fall. The invisible fingers held him tightly. He didn't let go of his grip on Riv's hand, though, nor did Kam. She unwrapped her arm from the beam. The ghostly fingers tugged them gently back toward the gap in the wall. Jake couldn't see behind him, but then he felt real hands grab him and pull him in. Equally firm and strong hands reached out as soon as he was through the hole to draw in Riv and Kam.

The invisible fingers relaxed, and Jake staggered to his feet. His father's arms held him up, and he grinned back at him. His father gave him a wink. Then he looked at the Bajoran boy and Cardassian girl, who were being helped to their feet by Odo and one of his men. Slapping his communicator, he called, "Sisko to Kira: What's our status?"

"It was just a warning shot, Commander," her voice reported. "It was meant to hurry up our search for his daughter. Shields took the blow. No damage and no casualties."

"There almost were," Jake's father said. "Tell the Gul

that he almost succeeded in killing his own daughter, but that we have her and she's safe. Sisko out."

Jake stood beside Kam and Riv. The Bajoran didn't seem able to raise his face to look at the others. "Are you going back to your father?" Jake asked Kam.

"I don't have any choice," she told him miserably. "If I don't, he'll attack this station." She looked at Jake's father. "I can't ask you to let me stay now. It wouldn't be fair."

The commander nodded. "You're a very brave girl. What will your father do when you get back?"

She shrugged. "He'll probably kill me. I've embarrassed him in public by running away. He knows I wasn't kidnapped, whatever he says."

Riv stared at her now. "You'd go back to him? Even knowing you're gonna die?"

"I don't have any choice," she said sadly. "If I don't, he'll blow up Deep Space Nine, and everyone will die."

Riv swallowed. "I was really wrong about you, wasn't I?" he managed to say. "You're braver than I am—and a whole lot nicer, too." His face set in a severe frown. "And I won't let him hurt you."

Nog snorted. "I don't see what we can do."

Riv grinned. "She may be braver and nicer than me, but I'm obviously still smarter than all of you. I've got a plan."

Odo glared down at them all. "This," he said, "I've got to hear."

Major Kira glanced up from the main control panel in obvious relief. On the main screen Jake saw Kam's father. Just looking at him made Jake shudder. Ashley gave a cry of pleasure and started across the room toward them, T'Ara following behind.

Jake, Nog, and Riv moved quickly to intercept them. It was vitally important that neither of them give anything away. "It's okay," Jake said loudly for the benefit of the Gul. "We're fine. She didn't hurt us." With his back to the screen, he held a finger to his lips, hoping they'd follow his lead. If only Riv's plan worked . . .

For a second it looked as though Ashley might say something. Thankfully, T'Ara caught on immediately. "We were most worried about you both," she said. "I am glad you are safe." Then she gave a wink before going stone-faced again.

"What is going on?" Gul Gavron demanded. "Did you rescue my daughter?"

"Daughter?" Jake's father asked, putting as much anger as he could into his voice. "Then you accept responsibility for her actions?"

"Actions?" the Cardassian echoed, puzzled. "What are you talking about? She was kidnapped."

"Kidnapped?" Commander Sisko shook his head. "You know that isn't true. She's a *spy*. And *she* kidnapped my son and his friends to try to hold them hostage."

Gul Gavron's eyes widened in shock. "She *what?*"

Taking her cue, Kam stepped forward, a meek expression on her face. "I'm sorry, Father," she said. "I was just trying to make you proud of me. I was wrong."

This was obviously not what the Gul had been expecting at all. "What do you mean? What did you do?"

Kam took a deep breath. "I wanted to be a good daughter to a Gul, so I stowed away on a freighter heading here to Deep Space Nine. I've been hiding out for a week, trying to learn the weak spots. I thought I'd make you proud of me by being a good spy, but I kind of screwed up, didn't I?"

Gul Gavron's face furrowed in a frown. "And you took *all three* of those boys hostage?"

Kam spread her hands helplessly. "I didn't know what else to do. When the guards came after me, I panicked. I thought they'd come to arrest me, not to tell me you were here. So I took hostages."

"Well!" Gul Gavron was starting to look almost proud.

Jake's father glared up at the screen. "She's a criminal and a spy," he declared loudly. "If it were up to me, she'd spend most of her life in prison. However, in the interests of peace, I will allow her to return to you. I insist that she be treated as a criminal and punished very severely. Is that understood?"

"I understand, Commander," the Cardassian replied. "But you have no authority over me. I shall deal with her as I see fit. Now—send my daughter back!" He switched off the viewer.

Odo gave a sharp bark of a laugh. "A wonderful piece of acting, Commander," he said. "I almost believed you myself."

"The question is," Jake said, worried, "did *he* believe it all?"

Riv snorted. "Are you kidding? He bought the whole thing." He gave Kam a grin. "The art of telling a really

106

good lie is to make sure it's what the person listening really wants to hear. He's gonna be as proud as anything of you for trying to be a spy."

Kam nodded. "And since the commander *insisted* that I be punished, he'll treat me better than normal, I think, just to show he can't be bossed around." She sighed. "I hate telling such lies, even to him, but what else can I do?"

"Nothing," Jake's father said. "They started with the lies. If you tell them what you really think, they would only punish you. That won't help anyone, will it?"

"No." Kam smiled wistfully. "I wish I could stay with you, but I must return. I won't forget any of you. I promise that I'll make sure that some Cardassians know the truth about what you're really like."

Riv grinned. "I bet you'll do it. I've got a lot of faith in you."

Ashley shook her head. "I'm missing something here. Riv *likes* you?"

The Bajoran punched her lightly on the arm. "Don't let it go to your head," he told her, "but even you've grown on me."

Kam moved across to the transporter pad. She gave them all a sad wave. "Goodbye," she called. "I promise I won't forget!"

"Goodbye!" they all chorused as she vanished.

A moment later Dax looked up from her science station. "The ships are moving away," she reported. "They are headed home."

"Good." Commander Sisko turned to Major Kira. "Cancel red alert. Odo, did your men find Riv Bothna?"

"Yes," the constable replied. "They're on their way here with him now."

"Fine." Jake's father looked down at the Bajoran boy. "There's just one thing to clear up now," he said.

Jake shook his head. "Two things, actually." He turned to Nog. "I think you'd better give Riv his earring back."

"It's mine," Nog insisted. "I found it!"

Riv's hand flew to his ear, and he reacted as he realized that he'd lost the relic of his parents. "It must have come off in the struggle," he said. "I'd forgotten about it with so much happening." He held out his hand. "Thanks for finding it for me," he said.

"It's mine," Nog insisted. "I found it; it's mine. That's the Third Rule of Acquisition."

Riv smiled slowly. "Then I guess I'll just have to pierce your ear so you can wear it," he said. He held up his fist and took a step forward.

Quickly Nog held out the earring. "Take it," he said nervously. "The Seventy-Sixth Rule of Acquisition says: 'Every once in a while, declare peace.'"

"Thanks." Riv took his treasure back and pinned it in place just as the turbolift arrived. Two of Odo's men pushed his uncle Bothna out of it and over to the commander.

"Commander Sisko!" Bothna said. He sounded on the verge of panic, but there was anger in his voice. "What has that evil little creature done now?"

Jake's father glowered at the fat Bajoran. "Kidnapping," he snapped. "Menacing. Endangering the lives of everyone on this station. I'm revoking his parole."

Bothna looked happy. "Then you'll throw him in jail where he belongs at last?" he asked.

"No." Odo smiled as Bothna's face went white with shock. "If you recall, when we last met, I told you I was releasing him into *your* custody. And that I was holding *you* responsible for his actions. I don't think you quite understand. *He* isn't being charged with those crimes— *you* are!"

"Me?" howled Bothna, on the verge of fainting. "But—but that's not legal!"

Odo smiled at the Bajoran. "No, I agree. But it *is* justice."

"You see," Jake's father explained, "I'm convinced that Riv has seen the error of his ways and given up his bad behavior. But I'm *not* convinced that you have. You have done nothing but complain about Riv. You've shown him no affection and no caring. Now, if I have your word that you will do your best to change and to try and give him a good home, then I'll let you out on probation—under Riv's care."

"And if not?" asked Bothna, trembling.

Odo smiled nastily. "Oh, about thirty years in a jail cell, I think."

"I accept."

The commander smiled. "I thought you might." He turned to Riv. "Do you think you can take responsibility for him?"

"Yes, sir," replied Riv. He looked up at his uncle. "Today I've learned that a lot of my ideas were way off target. Maybe my feelings about Uncle Bothna were, too. I promise I'll do my best."

The tubby Bajoran looked down at his nephew, a frown on his face. "You will?" he asked, hardly able to believe it.

"Yes, Uncle," Riv promised. "I'm sorry for everything I said to you in the past."

Bothna looked at him, and then at Commander Sisko. "Well, if even Riv can change, then I guess I can, too. I give you my word, Commander, that I'll do my best."

Jake's father smiled. "I can't ask for more than that. Good luck . . . both of you."

The two of them left Ops together. Jake's father turned to face his son. "Jake, I am very proud of what you did today. You and your friends helped a great deal in all of this."

Jake blushed. "Uh, thanks, Dad."

"However," his father finished, a little more severely, "this is still a school day. If you are not all down there within ten minutes, I shall recommend detention for the lot of you."

Jake looked at Nog, Ashley, and T'Ara. The four of them turned and fled. As they did so, they heard both the commander and Odo chuckling.

"I don't think he's really serious," Jake said as the lift took them down.

"Nah," agreed Nog. "Grown-ups just hate having to owe kids for anything."

"Back to school," said T'Ara. "It will seem awfully quiet now if Riv behaves and now that Kam has gone. I miss her." Then, as she realized that sounded suspiciously emotional, she added, "She presented an interesting opportunity to learn about the Cardassians."

"Yeah," Ashley agreed. "I'll miss her, too." Then she grinned. "On the other hand, *this* time when I fix the replicator, it's gonna *stay* fixed. No more stew and cheesecake—ever!"

"I don't know," Jake managed to say with a perfectly straight face. "I was actually starting to kind of like it. . . ."

About the Author

JOHN PEEL was born in Nottingham, England—home of Robin Hood. He moved to the U.S. in 1981 to get married and now lives on Long Island with his wife, Nan, and their wire-haired fox terrier, Dashiell. He has written more than forty books, including novels based on the top British science fiction TV series, *Doctor Who,* and the top American science fiction TV series, *Star Trek.* His novel, *Star Trek: The Next Generation: Here There Be Dragons,* is available from Pocket Books. He has also written several supernatural thrillers for young adults that are published by Archway Paperbacks—*Talons, Shattered, Poison,* and the forthcoming *Maniac.* He is working on his next Jake and Nog story, *Field Trip,* to be published next year.

About the Illustrator

TODD CAMERON HAMILTON is a self-taught artist who has resided all his life in Chicago, Illinois. He has been a professional illustrator for the past ten years, specializing in fantasy, science fiction, and horror. Todd is the current president of the Association of Science Fiction and Fantasy Artists and Illustrators. His original works grace many private and corporate collections. He has co-authored two novels and several short stories. When he's not drawing, painting, or writing, his interests include metalsmithing, puppetry, and teaching.

Beam aboard for new adventures!

A new title every other month!

Pocket Books presents a new, illustrated series for younger readers based on the hit television show STAR TREK: DEEP SPACE NINE®.

Young Jake Sisko is looking for friends aboard the space station. He finds Nog, a Ferengi his own age, and together they find a whole lot of trouble!

#1: THE STAR GHOST

#2: STOWAWAYS
by Brad Strickland

#3: PRISONERS OF PEACE
by John Peel

#4: THE PET
by Mel Gilden and Ted Pedersen
(Coming in mid-November 1994)

Published by Pocket Books

954-02